Always and Forever Until the End of Time

by

Dilys J Carnie

Always and Forever, Book 3

Always and Forever Until the End of Time

Cover Art by *The Wild Rose Press, Inc.*

The Wild Rose Press, Inc.
PO Box 708
Adams Basin, NY 14410-0708
Visit us at www.thewildrosepress.com

Publishing History
First Edition, 2024
Trade Paperback ISBN 978-1-5092-5417-0
Digital ISBN 978-1-5092-5418-7
Previously Published: 2018 Beachwalk Press

Always and Forever, Book 3
Published in the United States of America

Dedication

In August of this year, my daughter and her husband marked their fifth wedding anniversary.
They have been given the gift of two little boys, ages 3 years old and 10 months.
In May of 2024, my son will get married, and he already has a son who is four years old. I am blessed with three adorable grandkids. The way my daughter and son have developed into mature and loving parents makes me incredibly happy and proud.
Emma and Justin, Chris and Dani, May your love and strength for each other last Always and Forever until the end of time,
Love Mum xx

Prologue

Amelia Rose watched Tony from the bedroom window as he walked down the path. She thought he might turn around when he stopped at the wooden gate with his hand on the catch. But he only paused for a moment before he opened the gate and walked out of her life forever.

She wouldn't cry; it was impossible to squeeze out any more tears. Twelve months of her life had been spent with a man that she thought she'd loved. Enough time had been wasted over Tony Rossi.

Amelia turned from the window and walked away without a backward glance. Something akin to hate seared through her body, and she took her bag from where it was lying on the chair and opened it.

Taking out the diamond ring that had been on her finger, she looked at the shiny object, and a tear dropped onto her cheek, rolling down the skin until it disappeared. Amelia turned and opened the dressing table drawer and dropped the ring inside. That part of her life was over, and she didn't want a reminder of how stupid she'd been.

There was relief, sadness, and then anger at how she had been deceived and lied to. Now she would be invisible to a world she knew; a world that had been her life for twenty-two years. She no longer recognized the man who asked her to marry him. How stupid and naïve she had been. Tony had managed to get past the officers protecting her, and he'd given her forty-eight hours to disappear.

So much for protection!

For the rest of her life, she would be checking behind her wherever she went. That was the legacy she had been left to live with. That and the memory of seeing Angus Rossi kill a man in cold blood. That picture would be forever seared in the cortex of her brain.

Chapter 1

There was something very satisfying to her well-being living in Cape Charles. With just over a thousand people currently residing in this small community Amelia had felt safe from the first moment she'd stepped off the bus.

Everyone in town knew her as Amelia Bailey, not Amelia Rose. She had decided to keep her first name under the advice of her protection team. Amelia had to change her name and identity just over eight years ago when she'd left a very foggy London and never looked back.

There were far too many secrets about her past—scary, hushed, chilling parts of her life that she had managed to hide very successfully. But she'd never forgotten them for one moment; she never wanted to be too complacent.

When she had come into the UKPPS—the United Kingdom Protection Service, the equivalent to WITSEC here in the United States—she'd known that it would be a life of always looking over her shoulder, and that had been the case for a long time.

Four years ago she'd come across Cape Charles and fallen in love with this quaint town. After two years in the UK and another two traveling through America she finally thought it was safe to settle down. However it didn't stop her from sleeping with a baseball bat right

3

beside her at night.

As she shut her front door and locked it she could already feel the sun's warmth even though it was only eight-thirty AM. Amelia walked down her path, the coral pink flowers on her crepe myrtle scenting the air. The gracefulness of the multi-stemmed branches as they gently caressed each other in the light breeze made her breathe deeply.

Amelia loved her home, loved her life. She shut the small, white gate and made her way on foot the ten-minute walk she made five times a week to work. She didn't own a car, there was no need for one. The sound of a bicycle bell shrilled behind her as she walked on the pavement past Pine Street, and she turned around to see her neighbor.

"Morning, Amelia."

"Morning, Geoff." She smiled and waved to his disappearing back.

It had taken her a while to get used to being able to walk down this street without jumping every time someone or something came up behind her.

She'd had no family, no one who'd miss her, and she thought it should have been easier to give it all up, but it had been a lot harder than she'd ever imagined. But that had been eight years ago, and here in Cape Charles, she'd made a life for herself, one that had made her very happy.

Taking a right turn onto Strawberry Street, she strolled past Central Park. The flowing waters of the fountain were only one of the many attractions in the town's park. There was a large gazebo that had housed many a band. She liked to listen to the music at night while sitting on the grass.

In the distance, the sound of the train on the tracks gave a hearty chug of metal against metal as it made its way through Cape Charles. She loved the walk to work, and never took for granted the freedom she had, because she knew that in a single moment it could be gone.

Amelia hung a right onto Mason Avenue and opened the door of Lizzie's Coffee Shop. The tinkle of the bell was the only sound in the usually busy shop, but that would change in thirty minutes when they opened.

There was a café downstairs, which sold homemade muffins, cookies, and coffee. Upstairs was the home to hundreds of books. People could just sit in the shop and read them, or they could take books with them and leave one of their own in its place. The two large front windows let in the bright sunshine, allowing the several indoor plants to flourish.

Large, tan-colored sofas with bright yellow cushions looked comfortable and housed many a customer throughout the day. Small chairs and tables with cushioned pads on them made this more than just a coffee shop.

Lizzie was getting older, and it seemed that she relied on Amelia a lot more, but she didn't mind. Although there was a great support staff that had been with her boss for longer than she had. In the time they had worked together they had become good friends, and Lizzie was inclined to mother her somewhat…which was nice.

Amelia's love of books and the occasional muffin— well, perhaps more like a daily indulgence, she thought, chuckling to herself—made this her dream job. She used to be the ultimate party girl, but after her experience, she'd become much more reserved. She had grown up in a foster home, and in her youth she had been a little out-of-control. Amelia didn't remember her dad, but her mum was forever in her heart.

"Morning, Amelia. It's a beautiful day," her boss said as Amelia came around the counter and found the older woman on her knees, filling the cupboard with packets of coffee.

"For goodness sake, Lizzie. What on earth are you doing?" Amelia said as she dropped her purse to the floor and bent down to help her.

"I would have thought that was fairly obvious, my girl."

"What did the doctor tell you? No bending or lifting for at least another month." Amelia tried to be cross with her. After a recent hip replacement surgery, Lizzie had insisted on coming back to work.

"Sugar, I'm well aware of what Dr. Foster told me. The old codger should have retired years ago."

Amelia laughed as she helped Lizzie up. "That old codger thinks of you as more than a patient," she said, fully aware of how the doctor looked at her friend. As long as she'd been there, it had been like that. And yet Lizzie refused to see it that way.

When Dr. Foster tried to pass Lizzie along to the new doctor, she point blankly refused. Amelia knew why he'd tried to do that, and so did Lizzie. He wanted to ask her out, and of course, it wouldn't be ethical to go out with a patient, but Lizzie would not concede to let him do the right thing. Stubborn should have been her middle name.

"You either go sit down and rest for five minutes or I'm going to send you home," Amelia said.

"You're not the boss yet, young lady."

"You'll always be the boss, Lizzie, but I'm worried that you're doing too much." Wrinkling her brow, she watched as her friend took a seat in a nearby chair and closed what looked like very tired eyes.

Lizzie was a tall, elegant woman. Her snow-white gray hair was cut short and enhanced her facial features. She had flawless skin with just a few wrinkles.

She was the first friend Amelia made when she moved to town, and she cared for her very much. But Lizzie was stubborn, and for her to be sitting down when she had told her to, meant that she wasn't in top form. Because the Lizzie she knew would have taken zero notice of her. It worried her slightly, but she was sure that Lizzie was on the road to recovery.

She picked up her purse and went into the back to hang it on the hook and put her apron on. Yes, she could honestly say she was happy here, and she hoped that would never change.

****

Liam Miller needed this break away from his normal life. When his friend Jarrod had said he was working in Cape Charles and beleaguered Liam's male ego to fuck with comments about him having soft hands and muscles, Liam didn't think twice about answering the challenge to help his friend out with the job he was doing. The trouble with being a criminal law attorney was that you forgot what it was like to do manual labor.

After a hard, six-month case, he needed to erase work from his mind. Normally Liam had no problem going from case to case, but he'd come to a time in his life where he just wanted to re-address the uncertainty he felt about which road to take at the age of thirty-two. In the courtroom, he could be tenacious, and some would say an unyielding son of a bitch. But what was he really like? Did he even know himself, know if he was even capable of having a life without the aid of his work to help him?

He'd known Jarrod since he was fifteen. There were three of them, Max being the other musketeer in their group. All three had been in the same children's home and had stuck together like glue. Through all their troubles, near misses, and doubts they had remained the best of friends.

Liam had been in Cape Charles a week and was staying at a hotel not far from where Jarrod was doing some work for a friend of theirs who'd just had a new house built. A massive kitchen that his friend had designed, some walk-in closets, some flooring in the master bedroom and spare rooms. There was no denying that it would look awesome. Jarrod was an amazing carpenter, and the men he had working for him certainly knew how to work with pine wood. Jarrod could have had his employees do the work, but he liked to be more involved than sitting in an office giving orders. On more than one occasion Jarrod had been mistaken for a worker rather than the boss.

Liam had found this coffee shop, and it wasn't so much the beverage he liked but the woman who served him. She was a little standoffish, but he couldn't stop looking at her auburn curls and beautiful green eyes.

The first time she had asked, "How can I help you, sir?", the way she said *sir* from those pale pink lips made his abs tighten as he'd just done a hundred sit-ups. Her voice held an accent he couldn't quite place.

Her hair was always up in a bun, but a few curls would slip out on their own accord. She was such a beauty, but her face held a story that she tried to hide. He didn't know what it was, but then again, didn't everyone have a few secrets?

Liam sauntered down Mason Avenue, and there was a certain amount of anticipation in his step as he neared the café. She made him feel alive by just looking at him. Hell, he only had to think about her and he felt animated. The black apron she wore and the counter she stood behind had hidden what her body was like, but he just knew it was sexy like she was.

He saw her through the window before he went in, and shoved his hands into his jeans pocket and watched her laugh at something the other woman behind the counter said to her. A caring hand lay on her arm, and he could tell that they were close.

As she turned back to serve a customer, she looked straight at him, and just like that, the laughter receded. Although she didn't look away Liam felt the distance almost immediately. And despite the warm September weather he felt a chill inside him. Something had happened to her. He'd come across enough cases involving fear to see that.

The café was full of people, all milling around, but he only had eyes for her.

"Stop gawking at the redhead and get the coffee," a voice said behind him.

So intent was his concentration on said redhead that he almost jumped out of his still-new work boots.

"Jesus, Jarrod, you almost gave me a heart attack."

His friend, who was slightly smaller than his six-foot-four height, stood beside him with a smirk on his face.

"Now I know why you take so long to get the coffee

9

and muffins every morning." The sound of comical sarcasm filled Jarrod's voice.

"Ha!" he said because he didn't know what else to say since it was true that he was preoccupied.

Jarrod was happily married to Maisy and they'd just had a baby girl, Mia, which was even more poignant because his wife had lost her two children in a car accident when her ex-husband had been driving. It was a crazy house with Maisy's dog Elsa and the two puppies, Anna and David, but it was a warm, happy home; something that he, Jarrod, and Max had never had.

They'd all been confirmed bachelors until Jarrod got married. Then Max had fallen for an English girl while on a business trip re-doing some of his aero designs for the British government. Now, Max, Talia, his new wife, and her nephew Charlie, who was five years old, were a family.

Liam had yet to meet the right woman. Now in his early thirties, he realized that it just might not be in the cards for him. He'd always said that he was happy and marriage wasn't for him. But after seeing his two best friends slip into the sanctity, he could see that his tunnel vision had come from his past. Many of his associates used the word *divorce* as if it was a natural occurrence...almost as if they married expecting it to happen.

A dig in the ribs brought him back to reality. "Ouch," he said as he rubbed where Jarrod had caught him. "Fuck, what was that for?" Liam asked, pretending that it had hurt him.

"Stop staring at the poor girl."

He didn't realize he was still looking at her until he saw the pink bloom on her cheeks as she turned away to serve a customer. Liam followed Jarrod through the door, and the jingle of the bell made the woman he'd been staring at glance up from what she was doing. A slight dusting of freckles veiled a flawless skin, golden with the sun.

Her gaze met Liam's as they stepped up to the counter she was standing behind. There were all sorts of goodies behind the glass, but he couldn't seem to take his eyes off her. It was such a clichéd moment that he cursed himself for being all kinds of a fool.

He was behaving like a half-witted teen instead of a man who had plenty of experience with women. No wonder Jarrod was staring at him as if he'd grown an extra head. But being so close to her seemed to make his brain and body behave in an incredibly perplexing manner.

"What can I get you gentlemen?" she asked.

And before he could answer, Jarrod had ordered.

Damn it! He mentally shook himself and brought his focus to the here and now instead of in a daydream.

A few weeks ago he'd been knee-deep in a very intense trial where a woman had killed her husband, but not before he had broken both her arms, dislocated her jaw, and knifed her in a lung. He physically and mentally abused her for all their married life until she could stand it no longer. It was a long, hard case, because although Liam agreed it was wrong to take another life, this woman had been to hell and back, and no one deserved to be abused the way she'd been.

The poor woman had been so completely violated that her right to live a life without fear drove her to do something that had happened in an instant. It was abhorrent to even imagine what she had been going through.

He won the case, but it had been mentally and physically exhausting. It had been a pro-bono case, one of the many he did.

It wasn't a coincidence that she was given the job that he had told her about, or the apartment that was in her price range to rent. The satisfaction of being able to help her get her life on track had given him more pleasure than he ever would have imagined.

Yes, he gave to charities, several in fact, but to do something for a person where you could see the difference was immensely satisfying.

Glancing at Jarrod, Liam saw a bemused expression on his friend's face. "Why are you looking at me like that?" he asked.

"Because I've never seen you act like this before."

Liam shrugged his shoulders. "I have no idea what you're talking about."

"Buddy, you also don't normally lie."

Jarrod was right: he didn't lie…ever. However, he was usually very good at hiding his feelings. Jarrod was the only person who could see into his soul, and at times it was incredibly annoying.

When Liam's Aunt Jane had dumped him on the doorstep of the children's home, Jarrod and Max took him under their wing. Liam had waited for his aunt to return for him, but she never did, and eventually he'd given up waiting.

He had never known his mom. As far back as he could remember he'd lived with his alcoholic aunt. If he thought about it, he figured his aunt had done him a favor; at least he'd met Max and Jarrod, and they had encouraged each other to strive for a life that was better than they'd had. There was only one way he would have ended up if it hadn't been for his two friends—instead of putting people behind bars, he would have been the one being locked up.

"I'm not lying now, just looking at a pretty face," he said under his breath as the redhead handed them their coffee. "Thank you," he said as his fingertips touched hers.

"You're welcome," she said, pulling her hand away, and before he could say anything else she disappeared behind the beaded curtain.

"Come on," Jarrod said, raising his eyebrow. "Let's get you back to work before you start drooling all over the floor."

"Oh, shut up," Liam said as a grinning Jarrod opened the door for him.

Giving him a speculative glance, Jarrod gestured with his hand for Liam to go first. Liam flipped him off before stepping out into the sunshine and slipping his sunglasses from the top of his head to cover his eyes.

Fucking hell!

****

Amelia never took her freedom for granted. She knew that at any time it could be taken away from her. After all, one day Angus Rossi would be free, and if he was anything like the man she remembered, his time in prison would only have made him even more determined to come for her. He was not the type of man to forgive.

She'd spent the last eight years hiding from the life she'd left behind. It had been hard moving from place to place. The first few years she'd been terrified of her own shadow. Every time a person had looked at her intently, she'd felt the need to move on.

This life here and now had evolved into something that was almost liveable, except she was a different person. In as much as she respected herself and all that she had become, especially as she had no one who could give her advice regarding whether she was going down the right path.

What had she been like before her life had changed? Innocent, trusting, lonely! But that girl was gone, replaced with one who was always looking over her shoulder, alone because she was too frightened to forge any kind of relationship in case she had to move on.

So when for the last two mornings she'd been waiting for the café doorbell to jingle and the tall, handsome man to walk in and make his order it had surprised the hell out of her. Mostly because she hadn't felt that warm, fuzzy, unexpected feeling when your eyes locked with someone for a long time.

Anxious spots danced before her eyes, and she once again wondered who he was. She would have remembered him if he'd been local. The way he drew his hands through his already disorderly, sun-streaked, tawny brown hair was incredibly sexy. He had a gentle smile that shone through his sky-blue eyes fringed with the darkest of eyelashes.

Work…that's what she needed to stop her mind from wandering into territories that would not bode well for her way of life. The chatter of the customers she served and conversed with was enough for her to take her mind off the man.

It was five-thirty when she finally locked the coffee shop door and turned the *open* sign to *closed*. It had been a busy day, and she'd hardly had time to breathe. She'd sent Lizzie home early, although the woman had argued for what seemed like forever about how she was the boss and she was fine.

It was clear to Amelia that Lizzie was far from fine. Eventually, she managed to put her in Dr. Foster's car. He was not only Lizzie's doctor but they had gone to school together. He just happened to be in the café when Amelia had been trying to get her boss to go home. Sending her home had been far easier with a familiar face. Amelia sighed, knowing that tomorrow it would be the same argument.

Walking up the stairs to the book room, she tidied it up. She loved books and had always been a big reader. The way Lizzie had designed the shop was like heaven to her…coffee, cakes, and books, what wasn't there to like about working here? Picking up some plates and cups, she returned downstairs set them in the dishwasher, and turned it on.

After retrieving her purse, Amelia stepped outside the shop and locked the door. Turning around, she lifted her face toward the bright blue sky. She felt the warmth of the sun, and she took a deep breath of the fresh air before slipping her sunglasses on. Putting her purse strap over her head so that it fell across her body, she took a single step forward, then plowed into something hard.

But as she looked up, she realized that it wasn't so much *something* as *someone*. And although she was cautious of strangers, this guy had been coming in for coffee the last few days, and she'd become very adept at reading people.

She didn't fear him but was always aware that a friendly person could also be a dangerous one, especially with her past. He'd absorbed the impact and he had hold of her arms, preventing them both from tumbling to the ground. He smelled nice, woodsy with hints of amber, and the scent of him filled her senses.

For one second, she had a vision of being wrapped up in his warm arms but then shook herself at such a ridiculous thought. She hadn't had a relationship since Tony—once bitten, twice shy—and she'd decided that being on her own was the only way to live her life. It was lonely, but she'd gotten used to it...or she thought she had.

Cape Charles was a small place, and this man stood out. The reaction she was having to him made no sense at all. The way his light blue eyes were teasing her with their brightness told her that she was far too close to him, especially when her gaze was drawn to the dimple on his chin.

Twisting free of his hold, she stepped back. He let her go but watched her steadily while she swallowed and tried to get a hold of herself.

He bent to look into her eyes. "Are you all right?"

"Yes, I'm fine, thanks. Did I hurt you?"

"Not at all," he said, teasing her with a smile.

Amelia could feel the tension in her body and the quiver in her belly tighten. This was the weirdest encounter she'd ever had. She couldn't make out if it was just plain erotic, or if it had been way too long since she'd felt a man's arms around her.

His hand rested on her arm as he drew her against him to let someone pass. For an enjoyable moment, she stayed where she was as a rare sensation smoothed up her spine that was enticingly sexy. But that was just for a moment before Amelia pulled herself together and chastised her behavior.

There was nothing else to say, so she smiled at him

and walked away.

"Are you just going to walk away and not acknowledge what just happened between us?"

She stopped in her tracks turned around slowly and faced him. There was a small quirk on his mouth, but she couldn't see his eyes now as he'd put sunglasses on that she'd noticed had been hanging from the v of his dark blue t-shirt. They mirrored her reflection, and Amelia could see her own expression, one of sheer embarrassment.

"And what did you think happened?" she asked in her sternest voice, even though she began to feel a little heated. It was just due to the unusually warm evening…well, that's what she tried to tell herself.

There was a conspicuous air of charm that emanated from him, and she was certain that this man drew women to him like bees to honey. But she'd already been down that path with disastrous consequences, and just thinking about it shattered her. That was what had gotten her into a mess in the first place—a man with irresistible charm and her naïvety to men. She wasn't that girl anymore.

"I think you've been in the sun too long," she said.

"Uh-huh, is that what you think?" he asked as she once again tried to make her way home.

Her pace was a little faster as she continued down the street before making a left onto Strawberry Street. She breathed out a sigh as she walked along the path which took her home.

Amelia froze for a split second when she felt someone beside her until she realized it was the coffee man.

"Excuse me, are you following me?" she said as she stopped and looked at him.

"If I said yes, would it freak you out?"

Did it? For a moment she just stared at him. He stood with his hands pushed into the pockets of his blue jeans.

"Yes." She broke eye contact with him and continued toward her destination.

But he was still beside her. And although he could probably walk a lot faster than she could with his long legs, he matched her small steps.

"Do you find it hard to understand what I'm saying?" she asked as they walked past Central Park.

"No, although you do have an accent, which I can't place." He looked like he was waiting for her to elaborate, but she didn't.

She stopped suddenly and crossed her arms, making a point of looking right at him. "And?" She was getting slightly irked by him and his layered looks that she didn't even want to understand.

"Meet me for a drink tonight?" he said with a smile. "And I'll turn away."

She bit her bottom lip. "And if I say no?"

Amelia didn't like the way the conversation was going, and she didn't date, not since her last disaster, which had changed her life. Ever since that time she had repressed any kind of attraction she'd felt toward the opposite sex.

"No is no," he said. "For today. But tomorrow is another day."

She breathed out a sigh of relief.

"I can see you're going to take more persuading," he said with a mischievous grin. He seemed to enjoy her struggle to capture her composure.

"Well," she said ambiguously, "good luck with that."

He chuckled.

"See you," she said over her shoulder as she carried on walking.

"You can be sure of that," his deep voice came after her. "Coffee tomorrow morning."

She felt a little bit of pleasure spread over her and looked forward to making him coffee more than she'd like to admit.

Chapter 2

Liam scrambled for his jeans, which were lying in a heap on the floor where he'd left them last night. His phone was ringing, and he fumbled with it as he pulled it out of his pocket.

"What?" he grumbled as he lay back in bed and held it to his ear.

"Good morning, sleepy ass."

He looked at his watch. "Jesus, Jarrod, it's seven-thirty on a Sunday morning."

"And?"

"I thought it was a day off?" Liam drew his fingers through his hair, irritated by his friend's sarcastic tone.

"Did you read my text that I sent last night?"

"No."

"Well, if you had, you would have seen that the owners want the house finished a week early."

Lam had returned to DC to deal with some paperwork that had needed his attention and had crawled into bed at two-thirty AM.

Holy fuck!

"Get some pants on, buddy, or I'll be going for coffee myself and you won't get to see the hot redhead that you have an eye for." There was a distinct mockery in his tone, and Liam muttered a few choice words under his breath and hung up to the laughter at the other end.

He grabbed a quick shower, got dressed, and

bypassed the scent of bacon when he proceeded past the dining room of the hotel where he was staying. The blue sky was cloudless, and the sun was already shining. It surprised him that in September it could still be this warm.

The sound of hammers knocking, the whirl of saws, and the music from the radio told him that he was the only one of the crew not working. He didn't get paid enough to be here on a Sunday. Fuck, he wasn't being paid at all.

Liam heard voices as soon as he walked into the house. He had a blue t-shirt on that had *Steel Homes* embroidered on the top right-hand side, which all of Jarrod's employees wore, and working jeans. It was different from what he normally wore to the office.

You wouldn't think that Jarrod owned a multi-million-dollar business that he had built from nothing. He just looked and acted like everyone else on the worksite.

When they had shared a room with Max, their other friend, at a foster home they'd all had dreams, all had ideas on what they were going to do. And through hard work and determination, each one of them had made it to where they had wanted to be in their professions.

His eyes were hidden behind sunglasses, Jarrod turned his head when Liam approached. "Oh look, it's the part-timer," Jarrod said in a bantering manner.

"I didn't get back to town until two-thirty this morning, and I didn't check my texts, just crawled into bed."

"Why so late?" Jarrod asked.

"Hey, Geoff, haven't you got a home to go to?" Liam joked with the supervisor on-site as he came out of the makeshift office.

"Home, what's that?" The middle-aged man chuckled.

Liam picked up the conversation with Jarrod. "There was an accident on 64 East, and the back-up was huge."

Liam poured coffee from the pot that had been set up in the unfinished kitchen. He gulped a mouthful down and sighed at the pleasure it brought him.

"Well, while you were getting your beauty sleep the pine for the kitchen cabinets was delivered at five-thirty this morning and is now ready for my guys to start." Jarrod continued talking as they walked across what was the laundry room but now served as their makeshift office.

Jarrod took the roll of blueprints from the windowsill and put them on the large table they'd brought in there. He unrolled the prints and set his cup on one side to stop them from inrolling and took a hammer from his belt and set it in the other corner. Liam sat on a trestle as the sound of men working was prevalent with cursing as instructions were shouted above the noise. There was a distinct smell of sawdust, which was always evident in Jarrod's work truck.

"The builders are almost finished, which means we can get started upstairs, and the kitchen will be the last project on the list." A frown was etched into Jarrod's brow as he flicked through the blueprints.

"What's the problem?" Liam asked, going over to stand by him.

"Problem is Emily wants to change the layout for the walk-in closets, which is proving to be a bit of a predicament."

"Umm, and we know that David is so besotted with her that he lets her do whatever she wants," Liam said fondly.

They were friends of Jarrod's, but Liam had gotten to know David through some contract work he'd written up for him.

Liam looked at the drawings on paper that Jarrod had designed. "What if we just move that wall? It's an internal one and shouldn't change the layout that much."

"Exactly what I was thinking." He clapped Liam on the shoulder. "We'll make a carpenter out of you yet."

Liam was amused. "Not unless you up the pay."

"You don't get paid."

"Exactly."

"Tell you what," Jarrod spoke in a casual, jesting way. "I'll pay for the coffee and muffins when you go and see your redhead."

"Fuck off." Liam laughed. "She's hardly spoken to me," he said, not letting on about the conversation he'd had with her the other night.

A deep chuckle reverberated from his friend's chest. "Losing your touch, man, definitely losing your touch."

"Shut up," Liam said as he drained his coffee cup.

"So, how would you feel about knocking this wall down?" Jarrod rolled the blueprints up and put them under his arm.

"Show me the way. I need to be diverted from punching you on the nose."

****

Amelia was enjoying her day off, and she had decided to tidy up her pots of flowers. It wasn't a big space that she had, just a square of grass in the back which she had decorated with terracotta ceramic pots of color. The velvety, purple-ringed pansies with sporadic splashes of yellow and red took her breath away.

She was going to the park tonight to listen to the jazz group that frequently played in the gazebo. It consisted of five men and two women. They lived in Cape Charles but toured around the US playing their music. The men played the instruments and the women sang. Although sometimes the blonde female played the saxophone. The way that they combined each other's talents was what made them so good to listen to.

Amelia took her hat off and wiped her brow with the back of her hand. Jeez, it was hot today. Strands of her hair that had escaped her bun were sticking to the perspiration on her neck. She had to be careful with the protection from the sun. Her hair color and pale skin meant that she burnt easily.

Meow.

"Hey, baby girl. Are you hot too?" Amelia stroked the soft, gray fur of her cat Misty as she rubbed herself against her hand.

The cat had been a stray that had decided to call Amelia's home hers a couple of years after she had moved to town. When she took Misty in for a check-up and shots the vet informed her that the cat was about a year old. After putting up flyers everywhere, looking for the owner, she wasn't disappointed when no one answered them.

Looking at her watch, she decided she'd done enough for the day put away her tools and went inside. The cat followed her as she picked up the bag of dried food tipping some into her dish. Misty started crunching at it straight away.

Amelia went to the refrigerator to take out a jug of

homemade lemonade. Pouring some into the glass she'd picked up from the sink drainer. Amelia hadn't realized how thirsty she was, and she gulped the drink down, before holding the cold glass to her forehead. It helped to cool her down somewhat.

Typical…the AC wasn't working, and at the moment she didn't have enough money to call someone out to repair it. The house was just meant to be a pit stop, but after a few years she was given the chance to buy it at a ridiculously low price and she couldn't resist. She convinced herself that maybe—just maybe—she was safe there and wouldn't need to leave. But now, being the homeowner, she was responsible for all repairs and maintenance.

The house was like an oven, and even at five p.m., it hadn't seemed to cool down at all. The thought of a nice, cool shower had her hurrying through the living room to the bedroom.

Her little house was just one level, and she had a family bathroom but also an en-suite, which was what she mostly used. Removing her clothes as she walked through her bedroom and into the bathroom, she stepped into the cubical and turned on the water.

The spray was warm as it traveled over her body, and just for a moment, she luxuriated in it. The steam from the shower was thick and filled the air as the water washed away the grime of the day.

Picking up her shower gel from the basket that hung over the glass door, she squeezed the liquid onto her sponge and soaped herself, loving the scent of coconuts. Amelia tried not to think about the stranger who came in for coffee and muffins, but how could she not? What was there not to like? He was tall, handsome, and funny.

But she'd left relationships behind her. The fear and hurt from her last one still echoed in her heart, and she wasn't sure she'd ever be able to trust a man again. He'd come into the shop several times, and while he'd waited for his coffee she was aware of his stare and the tiny tingle of excitement she felt.

But when he stopped her on her way home, Amelia had become a little wary. What if Angus Rossi had finally found her? She knew that he had the contacts and the power to do that. The dread of that repeatedly clouded over any happiness she found. It was always there on the sidelines, reminding her that nothing was ever as it seemed.

Amelia had been unable to resist looking at the beauty of the man who had caught her eye when he came in for coffee, from his tawny-brown hair that ruffled in the breeze to his compelling blue eyes to the adorable dimple right in the middle of his square chin. He obviously took great care of his body, but there was a ruggedness and power in the way he stood that was appealing to her inner womanhood. And there was no ignoring the air of command and authority his presence held.

She rinsed the shampoo from her hair and lightly conditioned its length. Her long, auburn hair had a slight wave to it, so more often than not she just let it dry on its own. Turning off the shower, she stepped out and grabbed the large, pale yellow towel that was dangling from the rail. She wrapped it around herself then reached for a smaller towel and used it to rub her hair and squeeze out the wetness as she stepped back into her bedroom.

Opening the drawer to her pine unit, she took out some pretty, white lingerie and put it on. She stepped over to the wardrobe, opened the two doors, and considered what to wear.

It was still warm, so she pulled out a periwinkle blue, floral, summer shift dress that fell just a little smidgen above her knee. Taking it from a hanger, she stepped into it, and spreading her hands over her hips—which were in her mind too big—she smoothed the dress down and turned around to look in the mirror on the back of the wardrobe door.

Her reflection looked back at her. Eight years ago she would have been out eating dinner at some swanky restaurant, surrounded by people she neither knew nor liked. But it was her fiancé they wanted to be with, the man who knew how to make money.

Oddly enough, she had never questioned how much money he had. She just thought that his jewelry shops were doing well. Her innocent mind never realized that he was part of a family that was known for the way they did business, and not in a manner that was on the good side of the law.

It didn't take Amelia long to get the picture as clear as daylight that she just looked good on the end of his arm as she stood by him at functions she hated. Tony drew people to him with his good looks and personality that lit up a room, and that was what she had fallen in love with.

It was only later that she realized he belonged to one of the most prominent mafia families in London. The Rossis.

The relationship with a man who she thought was the love of her life slowly dwindled as she became more aware of what the family stood for. At the age of twenty-one, she had been sucked into a world she knew nothing about, but Amelia had loved Tony and had been blinded by that love.

She stepped away from the mirror. No one would ever know how terrified and alone she had felt when she'd seen with her own eyes what Tony's family was capable of. She had found herself in a position that would affect the rest of her life.

Amelia systematically got by minute to minute in the beginning. Now she could say that she only thought about her previous life day to day. However, she never became too complacent at how simple and lovely things were for her now.

No one here knew of her life before she came to live in this community, not even Lizzie, who had become her friend.

Meow.

She bent down and lifted the gray ball of fluff, then rubbed her face against the cat's head before setting her on the bed. Misty purred and pawed with her claws at the soft throw until she finally collapsed in a heap of total pleasure.

Heading to the bathroom, Amelia took her makeup bag from the drawer unit and put on a little mascara. She brushed her teeth before slicking some lip gloss over her lips. Returning to the bedroom, she picked up her tote bag, which contained a blanket for her to sit on and a bottle of water. It might get a little cooler later, so she slipped a cardigan in there as well.

The walk to the park only took five minutes, and she went through the gates and headed to the center where the gazebo was. This part of the park was already filling up with people. Usually she would find Lizzie and sit with her, but as her friend was still recovering from surgery and couldn't attend because she was unable to sit or stand for too long, Amelia was happy to pick a spot and sit on her own.

Spreading the blanket, she slipped off her sandals, sat down, and waited for the band to start. She watched while the various instruments were moved into position. A few people waved at her, customers that came into the shop, people she knew but not on a personal level.

The Java Seven started to play one of her favorite songs, Nina Simone's *Feeling Good,* with the blonde female taking on her role with remarkable talent. Amelia settled back to what was going to be a great musical evening and let herself be lulled into the moment.

****

Liam sat on the bed in his hotel room. Leaning against the pillows, he propped himself up. He rolled his shoulders. Damn, he'd forgotten how manual work hurt when you weren't used to it. He was fit and worked out every day, but his muscles were complaining…a lot. So he'd taken a shower to try to ease away a day of hard work and was now going through some emails on his laptop.

Jarrod had gone home to Nags Head to see his wife and baby, leaving Liam a list of jobs to get through. He looked at the tool belt he'd taken off earlier. Max and Jarrod had given it to him as a joke when he'd told them he was going to help with the rebuild in Cape Charles.

The two of them thought they were hilarious. He disagreed. And they roared even more. Sons of bitches thought they were so damned funny!

"Does he know how to use those tools?" Max had joked.

He'd joked along with them, because he had no idea,

29

and he'd chuckled to himself.

"Smart asses," he murmured under his breath as he scrolled through an email that needed his attention.

He was the first to admit that he had no handyman skills at all. Now give him a deposition to write or ask him to stand up in court and defend someone, and he was your man.

He worked deftly across the small keyboard with no hesitation in what he wanted to write, and in no time at all he had completed what was necessary until he got back to the office. Flipping the lid shut, he set the laptop on the nightstand.

He stood up and went over to open the window. His eyes drifted to the horizon where the sun was sinking fast. A beautiful lull of reds, yellow, and orange encapsulated the sky. Its reflection to the west of the Chesapeake Bay waters was mesmerizing as it glistened like a mirror.

His ear caught the sound of music, and he turned his head to the right where he could see lights on in the park by the gazebo. He looked at his watch. It was almost eight-thirty PM. Fastening the button on his jeans, he went over to the dresser and pulled out a t-shirt. He picked up his wallet and keys stepped out of his room and headed downstairs.

He enjoyed jazz, and it was better than sitting in his room on his own like billy-no-friends. There was a slight breeze as he walked through the gates to the park, but it wasn't cold. There was a large crowd of people in front of a group who were singing and playing various instruments. Some had brought chairs, but most were sitting on blankets.

Liam stood for a moment, listening to the group play

John Coltrane's *Blue Train*. He'd first gotten into jazz when he'd worked in a bar not far from George Town Law where he'd been studying his first year. They'd played old jazz, and he'd found that he really liked it, and ever since it had stayed with him.

He had an original album of Miles Davis and John Coltrane's *The Final Tour*. Liam loved vinyl, and his collection was substantial and worth a lot of money.

In his daily work as a criminal law attorney, he saw many examples of how people lived out their days and the ravages it brought to the people they loved. So it was nice to go home at the end of the day put something on his record player and unwind.

Folding his arms, he stood where he was until the band finished. Everyone stood and applauded, and rightly so, the group was good. It was interval time, and he watched some of the crowd disperse to the hot dog vendors. But his gaze was drawn to one person sitting on her own, opening the top of a water bottle.

The woman from the coffee shop.

She had the same impact on him as she had the first time he'd seen her. Even when she played hard to get the other night it hadn't deterred him one little bit. But there was something about her that tugged at him. He wasn't sure what he could read in those eyes…it looked like fear, and he hoped he was wrong, because he didn't want to think of anything bad happening to her.

Liam felt like a stalker just standing there and staring at her, so he made his way toward her. He knew the minute she recognized him. He tried to gauge her reaction, but she was very good at not showing how she felt; someone who was used to camouflaging her thoughts and emotions.

She nodded at him as he approached, and she screwed the top back on the bottle and put it into her bag.

"Hello. I thought it was you," he said as she leaned her head further back to see him.

"Indeed," she said dryly.

"I've just arrived here. I heard the music from my hotel room."

She nodded. "It's a great group. You've missed half the concert."

"I'm just in time for the second part?"

"You are."

"May I share your spot?" he asked, being forward because he knew for certain she would never ask him.

She wrinkled her nose, silent for a second. "Of course. Please sit down." She motioned with her hand at the space to the left of her.

"I'm Liam," he said and smiled.

"It's nice to meet you...again."

She wrinkled her nose, which he found endearingly sexy.

"I'm Amelia."

"A lovely name..." He hesitated for a second. "For a pretty lady."

She blushed a little bit at the compliment. "Thank you."

They were quiet for a moment as he settled on the blanket, but it wasn't a strained silence. It felt comfortable even though he could feel a tension in her body. She wore no makeup except black mascara over thick lashes and some gloss across her lips. It was hard to take his eyes from them. Despite the chatter around them, he could hear her steady breathing, almost in unison with his.

"Is this a local group?" he asked her.

"Yes." She nodded, looking up at him. "The Java Seven originated from here, but they play all over the country."

"This is a fabulous park," he said as he looked around at the well-laid-out area. The gazebo had an array of rainbow-colored lights now that the night was drawing in. He could see lights in the distance. "What's that?" he asked.

She turned her head and her auburn curls moved with her.

"That's the tennis court. There are still people playing," she said, turning back to him. "And on the other side is a large area of the park devoted to kids."

He smiled at her. She had this cute way of wrinkling her nose, which was slightly covered in freckles. But it was her eyes that kept drawing him in.

"Do you know the history of the park?" she asked him.

"No. I don't know much about Cape Charles at all."

"It's fascinating how it was constructed." There was delight in her voice. "In the late 1880s, the streets were designed around the park, although the park itself wasn't developed for a long time after that."

Liam nodded. "It's often the other way around, but I profess not to know much about design. It's my friend Jarrod who is the expert in that."

"Is he the one that sometimes comes with you for coffee?"

"Yeah, he's doing some work on a friend's house. He's a very good carpenter. Steel Homes is his business. I'm just helping out."

Amelia nodded. "So, do you help him all the time or

do you have another job?"

"I'm a criminal law attorney in Washington, DC."

"That must be interesting."

"Always, mostly hard work and a lot of satisfaction," he said, remembering his last case.

Amelia wrinkled her nose, and the freckles were like kisses from the sun. There was something slightly discombobulating about her, but he couldn't put his finger on it.

"I can see you in a suit and fighting battles in the courtroom," she said, smiling.

"As opposed to a tool belt and a drill you mean," he said laughingly.

"Oops, I think I'd better not say any more in case I get into trouble. I'll carry on with the history lesson." A smile crinkled her mouth. He could see how teasing her eyes were, and he chuckled, loving how she razzed him. "When the high school opened in the early 1900s," she continued, "the park served as a place for athletics and baseball. But when the schools were consolidated about thirty years ago, the park was closed."

He noticed that when she spoke she gestured with her hands to make her point. He could tell she was enthusiastic about it.

"How long have you lived here?" he asked.

"Four years," was all she said. Her expression was tight, but only for an instant. It was quickly replaced with the neutral one she normally had. He got the feeling that she didn't like talking about herself.

She glanced at him under long, dark lashes. He knew that she wasn't purposely using the look to make him hot, but it did.

"Do you come here often?" he asked.

"All the time. It's a great place to walk. And I love the music concerts. At this time of year, everything is so pretty."

"It certainly is." Liam studied her as she spoke, and for a moment he saw happiness in her face; it made her glow. "So, when did the park re-open?" he asked.

"Actually, not until 2010 when a group of residents came up with an idea called 'design your own park day', then a local architect drew all the ideas together, and this is what you see now." She gestured around her with her hands. "It opened with lots of pomp and ceremony, and quite rightly so. It was a great achievement for the residents of Cape Charles. There's a fabulous motto about the park—it takes a town to grow a park—and that's exactly what happened." Her voice was gentle, with a slight huskiness which he found very sexy.

The group returned and they both turned to face the front. The sound of hushed silence filled the air while the crowd waited for the music to start, and for the first time in a while he could feel his body relaxing.

Liam couldn't remember a time when he had felt so naturally stress-free. And sitting with Amelia, who was very easy to be with, he was happy just being there with her.

****

Amelia drew in a quiet, deep breath as Liam stretched his long legs in front of him. For a big man, he was surprisingly agile as he took up the rest of the space on her blanket. They were almost shoulder to shoulder, and regardless of how she had lived her life for the past eight years, this man made her stomach flutter and gave her skin goose pimples, and she shivered.

"Are you cold?" he whispered as the music started.

"Just a little." She reached into her bag drew out her cardigan and Liam took it from her and set it around her shoulder. She let out a long, silent breath as he helped her. "Thank you." She smiled at him.

"My pleasure," he said, arching an eyebrow.

Good God, the man was just too sexy for his own good, or hers. He made her forget about reality, and that wasn't good. It had been a lengthy time since she'd let any man get near her, and Liam would not be the exception.

It was only minutes before she was immersed in the wonderful world of Etta James and John Coltrane. She hadn't been this comfortable in a while. How strange it was to feel that way now. What was so different?

Amelia remembered a time when Tony had made her feel that way. She missed the company of a man, there was no use denying that. It had been a damn eternity without sex. Not because she didn't want it, but because she didn't want to get involved...and besides, she had a little sex toy that did just the job.

She'd gotten used to being on her own. Yes, the thought of marriage and children had crossed her mind on more than one occasion. But what kind of life would that be for a family? Putting their lives at risk was something she couldn't even think about.

At least with it just being her she could pick up and go at any time. And there would be a day when that would come. She did not doubt that one day Angus Rossi would be released from prison, and he would come looking for her. The thought that he might find her still tore at her insides and in her heart.

It was dark apart from the lights around the gazebo, and when the group finished their last cover, there was riotous applause as everyone stood up. Liam was up before her and offered his hand to help her. Amelia hesitated for longer than she should have, and she noticed a frown between his eyes.

She placed her hand into his slightly roughened one, and his long fingers wrapped around hers. It was as if everything was happening in slow motion, and as he drew her up she looked up into his face.

The silence between them was almost deafening, and she couldn't control the spasmodic trembling within her. His eyes glowed like stars, bright and glassy, and it was hard for her to tear herself away. But she did, releasing his hold. She crouched down to gather the blanket, which he had to step off, and folded it, returning it to her bag.

Liam leaned down and picked up her water bottle, and Amelia walked on ahead, not even looking to see if he was behind her. A hand settled on her arm before she could turn in the direction of her home.

"Are you running away from me?" he asked.

She looked up into his face and saw a devilish look come into his eyes. She tried not to look at that dimple, and she succeeded, but only because it was in her peripheral vision.

"Relax," he said as he took hold of her hand. "You'll be perfectly safe with me. Let me walk you home?" He must have felt the hesitation in her body, because he asked, "Do you want me to let go?"

And to show her he would, he loosened his hold, and she felt strangely bereft of his touch.

"Am I that scary?" His eyes were gentle as he looked down at her.

"No, of course not." She felt silly. She hesitated for

a moment, running all kinds of scenarios in her head.

What if he had something to do with the Rossis? What if they had found her? What if…

Oh good Lord, at some point she had to breathe and not think so much.

"There's an awful lot of something going on up there," he said as he brought up his other hand and tapped her forehead.

Jeez, wasn't that the truth? In a split-second moment that she hoped she wouldn't regret, Amelia tightened her hand around his.

He grinned briefly, his white teeth dazzling against his tanned skin. He returned the squeeze as they started to walk. "I'm assuming you're going to lead me in the right direction," he said.

"This is the way," she said, thankful that the full moon and street lights made it possible for her to see the way, not that she didn't know it like the back of her hand.

There were a few cars that passed them, and some people walking back from the concert, but all in all, it was a peaceful evening.

"So, Miss Mysterious, care to tell me a little bit about yourself?"

"I'm not mysterious," she said indignantly.

"Uh-huh, you are," he said with quiet emphasis. "I can't seem to decide on your accent…is there some British in there?"

"Very astute of you. Yes, I'm from London."

"And you like Cape Charles?"

"Correct." Her voice sounded cool and impersonal, even to her ears. "What else would you like to know?" she asked as they took the next right onto Bay Avenue.

Liam stopped suddenly. "I'm sorry," he said. "I

don't mean to pry."

"No, I'm sorry. I'm not used to talking about myself, and there really isn't much to know, but I didn't mean to be rude."

"You never have to tell me anything you don't want to, Amelia."

She nodded.

His mouth curved into a smile, and he used his fingers to raise her chin. "Okay?"

"Yes." She smiled in contentment, smelling the faint woodsy scent of his aftershave.

They started walking again, and she wanted to ask about him, but that would seem like double standards seeing she wasn't willing to talk about herself. So, they walked in easy silence, and very quickly they were at her home.

"This is me," she said, pointing at her little house.

"I had a nice time tonight," he said, still holding onto her hand.

"So did I." Every time her gaze met his, her heart turned over in response.

He looked at her as if he was scanning a picture in his mind. It should have made her feel uncomfortable, but it didn't.

"You're staring," she said, a breathiness in her voice.

"I can't help it. It's your eyes, they're beautiful."

She could feel herself blushing. It had been a long time since she'd let anyone get close enough to compliment her, and she didn't mind admitting it felt flippen damn good.

He didn't make her feel afraid or pushed into anything like the man who had hurt her so deeply, but she didn't want to be complacent either. Amelia checked herself as she swayed toward him and that whiff of his scent clouded her senses. She could get addicted to the smell of him.

Damn!

Amelia pulled back and turned, opening her gate, and walked up the path to her front door. She could feel him behind her but not so close that he was breathing down her neck. The outside light came on as she dug her keys out of her bag.

He put a hand on her arm, and she glanced at him over her shoulder.

"Goodnight. Thank you for walking me home." She spoke quickly as she put the key into the lock and opened her door, and for a moment, Amelia thought he wasn't going to move his hand, but after a split-second's hesitation he did.

"Why are you so frightened?" he asked her.

As she stood inside her doorway, Amelia twisted around to face him. He stood tall in front of her, and his body shielded her from the chilly night air. In the distance, she could hear the echo of an airplane, and nearer to her, the rustle of the crepe myrtles as they swayed together in the moonlight that shone through gaps in the branches.

"I'm not. Whatever gave you that idea?"

An image focused on her memory of the day she was told that if she didn't join the UK Protected Person Service it would be very likely that she wouldn't make it through the first twelve months without someone trying to kill her. She remembered very clearly how terrified that had made her feel.

Liam had a secondary instinct that seemed to allow

him to see in her what no one else saw. And that kinda made her feel uncomfortable.

They stared at each other for what seemed like the longest time. Liam narrowed his eyes, and she swallowed, trying to lubricate her dry throat. She thought he was going to question her again, but he just nodded.

"Okay, if you say so." He leaned forward and kissed her on the cheek before she could move away. "Thank you for a lovely evening. I enjoyed your company."

She cleared her throat so she could speak. "I had a nice time too. Goodnight." She could hear the huskiness in her tone.

Without giving him a chance to reply, she shut the door, immediately leaning against it.

"Holy fippen cow," she whispered.

Chapter 3

Liam had done a great deal of thinking last night, mainly because sleep eluded him. He couldn't stop the rush of excitement when he thought about Amelia. It wasn't just the way her wispy bangs fell against her forehead or the way a breeze kicked her curls. No, she had this inner beauty that shone through in an unmistakably genuine way. Plus, she was infinitely sexy.

There was a certain amount of vulnerability that she tried to hide, which made him want to protect her. Each time he tried to see into her eyes she'd drop her lashes quickly, as if she knew he was looking, and an inexplicable feeling of helplessness came over him, and he didn't like that at all. He was frustrated by the niggling sense of a problem that he couldn't recognize.

"Hey you, stop dreaming about the redhead." Jarrod pushed him as he passed Liam with a big grin on his face.

"Fuck off," Liam said as he pulled himself out of his thoughts.

Following his friend into the makeshift office, he crossed his arms as he leaned against the wall.

"How was everyone?" he asked Jarrod.

"They're great. Mia is cutting her first tooth."

"She'll be dating soon," Liam said, laughing.

"Not a chance." Jarrod scowled. "At least not until she's thirty-six."

Liam roared with laughter at the man's expression.

"You wait until it's your turn." Jarrod pointed his finger at him.

"Yeah, that's not happening anytime soon."

"Huh, we shall see!"

"So, what have you planned for me today?" he asked the man who had come back from his family visit with a spring in his step.

Jarrod arched his dark eyebrows mischievously. "Coffee and muffin run," he said. "Because by the looks of you, that's all you're up to today."

"You're a sarcastic son of a bitch," Liam said with a chuckle.

"You bet I am. Payback for the rough time you gave me when I met Maisy."

"Fair point," Liam agreed. "But this is nothing like you and Maisy," he said, trying to accept as true the words that had just come out of his mouth.

"Hey, buddy, if that's what you want to believe…but you know that's hogwash."

An image of Amelia standing in the porch light lingered in his mind for a moment, and he couldn't focus on what Jarrod was saying.

Jeez. He stood up quickly, almost knocking over the ladder next to him that had an open can of paint on it. He managed to catch it just before it splattered all over him.

Jarrod howled with laughter as he left the room, throwing over his shoulder the words, "In deep, buddy, in deep."

Liam shook his head in disgust. Max and Jarrod were both very happily married, and they'd been teasing him that his time would come. He had assured them that it would never happen to him. Love 'em and leave 'em—that was how he liked it.

Now he was acting like a sap over some woman he knew nothing about. What the hell was happening to his powers of common sense? He was baffled by his own behavior.

"Hey, are you going to do anything today?" Jarrod shouted at him through the joists that had yet to be covered.

"Yeah, on my way."

"Are you sure you can focus?" He heard a few chuckles from some of the crew.

This is going to be fun, he thought with a grimace as he made his way up the stairs to the top floor. He was going to be ribbed to high heaven. Good thing it was like water off a duck's back. He was tough, he could take it. After all, he could stand up to toughened criminals in court. How different would a few workmen be?

As he got to the top, there were four men, including Jarrod, and they were playing make-believe violins and humming the tune to *Romeo and Juliet*. Yep, this was going to be even harder than court.

"Idiots," he said as he pushed past them, laughing.

****

Amelia untied her apron. She was finishing early today. It had been a busy morning and she'd been rushed off her feet. She had kind of hoped to see Liam come in for his coffee, but there hadn't been any sign of him, and she was surprised to admit that it disappointed her.

Idiotic thought.

He was probably put off her after last night. She hadn't exactly been overly friendly. She was so used to pushing people away that it was hard not to be like that. Could she risk it, was it time to allow herself the pleasure of being intimate? Ten years since the court case and no one had managed to find her. Was she free to live a life, to be happy?

Amelia saw the car pull up outside the shop where she had been keeping watch. "Your taxi is here, Lizzie." Her friend was walking a lot better today, but not nearly well enough to be in the café all day.

"I think I'll send him away. I feel much better today."

"You most definitely will not," Amelia said as she got Lizzie's jacket and held it out for her to slip on.

"You're forgetting who is the boss here," she said as she pushed her arms reluctantly into the summer jacket.

"No, I haven't. I have clocked off. I'm being your friend."

"But they might need help."

"No, they won't, Lizzie. There are three people here, and if they can't manage, they have my phone number. I'm only ten minutes away."

Opening the door, she ushered her outside and into the waiting car. Lizzie scowled at Amelia, but she ignored the stare that would have sent another person into a withering wreck.

"Thank you for coming, Dr. Foster."

"No problem, Amelia. I'll sort her out."

"Amelia…" Lizzie was whispering, but Amelia ignored her and closed the door. She couldn't hear what her boss was saying, but by the way her lips were moving it wasn't something she wanted to hear. Amelia waved at the scowling woman and chuckled as the car drove away.

After checking to make sure the girls inside the shop were okay and she wasn't needed for anything, Amelia set off on her walk home. She attempted to shrug away the stiffness in her neck by breathing in the fresh air. It had rained through the night, and there was a scent of newly damp earth and wet grass.

Looking up into the sky, the blue that had been there yesterday was gone, and the rolling clouds were gray and dark. If she didn't get home soon, she was going to become very wet in the downpour that was on its way. So she hurried along at a quicker pace.

She was so tense that her shoulders hurt, and she could feel a headache coming on. Yesterday…was yesterday, and today she tried to forget the feeling of thudding in her chest when Liam had been so close to her.

Was she just being too complacent by thinking she could get involved with a man?

Just as she turned onto Bay Avenue her cell rang. She took it out of her raincoat pocket and looked at the screen.

Caller withheld?

She had thought it might have been work, but the display would have shown that. Clicking the button to answer, she put it to her ear and spoke.

"Hello," she said as she continued walking.

No one spoke.

"Hello," she said again.

Still no answer. She could tell someone was on the other end, although there wasn't a sound.

Without waiting any longer, she hung up and put the phone back into her pocket. Amelia floundered a little as she walked up the path to her house. Biting her lip, she turned around and shuddered inwardly at the feeling of foreboding that just shot through her.

Amelia searched the area, but there was no one to be

seen. A few cars passed, but nothing unusual. Dipping her hand into her bag for her keys, she gave one more scan of the neighborhood before turning to unlock the door. She stepped inside, shutting the door behind her. After hanging her coat and bag on the hook to her left she turned and walked through to the kitchen.

Misty came to meet her. *Meow.*

"Are you hungry, baby girl?" she said in that silly voice she kept just for her.

Amelia took some food from the cupboard and tipped it into the cat's dish. Stroking the top of her head, she watched for a moment as the cat ate with such gusto it was hard to believe she'd only fed her a few hours before.

She chuckled. Misty brought her so much joy. She never questioned her decisions, was always there when she needed to talk, kept all her secrets, and kept her warm at night.

Amelia rolled her neck from one side to the other. She knew what that pain meant—migraine.

Cape Charles had opened its arms to her and made her feel safe, a place she could finally call home.

There was a part of her that was scared to believe she could have a life. To be able to have hopes and dreams, to allow herself to have faith in what she could do. As a teenager she had no confidence in her ability to do things. Her mum dying had a detrimental effect on her self-esteem. That's what happens when no one wants you, and that was why she'd gotten involved with Tony Rossi.

Amelia shook her head as she walked through to her bedroom so she could change into her yoga pants and a t-shirt. She had witnessed much more than she'd wanted to. Even now the scene was painful to think about. The physical pain of it was acute, and the terrible regrets she had assailed her in every way possible.

For a long time, she had felt trapped in the lies she now had to live with. She'd lost her identity, and it had taken her a long time to come to terms with the new one. As she stood by her bedroom window Amelia looked out onto the rain that was now coming down fast.

The trial had lasted for months. Then Tony had given her forty-eight hours to leave after she'd sent his brother to prison with her testimony. If she refused to go, she knew that her life would be in jeopardy; Tony had made that very clear.

Biting her lip, she put her hands in the pockets of her pants and stood for a long moment. The harsh realities of loneliness had long ago become a part of how she lived, afraid to become too close to anyone. Except for Lizzie, the woman who'd given her hope to carry on, somewhere she could be independent, someplace she could be familiar with.

Narrowing her eyes, she tried to focus on a movement across the road. Probably just old Mr. Harris. Frowning, she moved closer to the window, her nose almost touching the glass. Was someone hiding behind the magnolia tree in his garden? She became increasingly edgy; the second time today she'd had that sensation.

A warning voice of uneasiness whispered in her head, and her heart started to beat a little faster. She left her room and went out the front door, not even bothering to put a coat on first.

The rain soaked her in seconds, but it didn't deter her as she walked across the road. It was a large tree, and the rain was bashing at the plentiful petals that were hanging from the branches, the heaviness of the waterdrops making them fall onto the neatly clipped lawn. Amelia stopped in her tracks. Suddenly her bravery seemed to vanish, and she didn't know what to do. Bits of hair were plastered around her face, and she clasped shaking hands in front of her.

"Amelia."

She heard a voice saying her name, but it seemed that she was glued to the spot and her feet wouldn't do what she wanted them to. Fear knotted inside her, and she gasped as a shiver of panic went through her body.

"Amelia." A hand on her arm startled her, and she turned around, ready to put the self-defense lessons to use, not that she'd ever had to do it before.

"Hey, hey…it's me."

Amelia came to a stop as she looked at Liam standing with his hand up to stop her. What the hell was she doing? *Oh my God.*

"Liam, I'm sorry. You startled me," she said shakily.

They stood there facing each other, dripping from head to toe as the rain stopped just as quickly as it had commenced, the sun peeping through the clouds. Instantaneously, she began to shiver and realized that she was cold and wet.

"Come on, let's get you inside. You're soaked."

He didn't touch her, just waited for her to walk with him back across the road to her house. For a moment she didn't move. Then, seeing the silliness of the situation, she hurried back the way she'd foolishly taken at a hundred miles an hour a few minutes ago.

What must he be thinking? She felt like such an idiot for letting her mind play tricks with her. Would this feeling ever leave her?

Amelia had been so certain she'd seen someone, so sure that it had something to do with her. But in reality, she was letting her mind work overtime.

She was always careful, that was the way her life was. Shit...she had become way too complacent. And she didn't like the niggling irritation of someone watching her across the road. As a wave of apprehension swept through Amelia it gnawed at her in a surge of fear that rioted within the confines of her mind in a momentary panic.

****

Liam closed the door and turned to face Amelia. She was dripping wet, her gorgeous red hair darker with the rain, and she pushed it from her face. Green eyes stared back at him with defiance, fear, and confusion, and he found that slightly disconcerting. She was afraid of something, but he had no idea what it was. However, now was not the time to ask.

"You need to go get out of those wet clothes and head into a hot shower," he said to her, expecting her to tell him to leave. But she didn't. She turned her back on him, and he assumed she was going to do as he'd suggested. "Amelia."

"Yes?" she said as she was about to close the door to what must have been her bedroom.

"Do you need any help?"

She shook her head. "No, of course I don't. I'm not a child," she retorted with a tinge of sarcasm.

That made him chuckle. He was happy to see that look of despair leave her face.

Despite the rain earlier the sun was shining through the window, and he walked from the front door where they had been talking into the kitchen area. He'd noticed how pale she'd been. What was she doing standing in the rain, just staring at that tree?

Liam looked around the small room. It was neat and compact, all in one, the living room to the left, and the dining room was part of the kitchen. He liked the design, the white cabinets, and the soft, neutral décor. It had a modern, spacious feel.

The blue marble effect counters were eye-catching, and she'd incorporated that shade into the curtains, living room, and eating area. It was designed carefully and everything was thought out exceptionally well. He went over to the coffee maker and set about making a pot of coffee. He found everything he needed very easily.

Liam stood with his hands in his pockets and looked out of the window into a tiny backyard and only some herb pots on the outside windowsill. He knew nothing about the plants and flowers that were in abundance at the front of the house. However, it was obvious that she did.

A small bang made him look down, and a cat came through the flap in the door. He went down on his haunches to stroke it. She was very pretty with striking markings. For a second, she was hesitant to respond to him, but not for long; she purred and pushed against his fingers.

"Hey, buddy. What's your name?"

"Misty."

He looked up to see Amelia standing by the doorway. Her hair was up but loose, silky strands fell over her shoulders. The style suited her. It was pretty and very sexy. She'd replaced her wet clothes with jeans and a pale green t-shirt. Her hands were clasped in front of her as if she wasn't quite sure what to expect.

"She's beautiful," he said as he stood up.

"Yes, she is, though she can be a little terror at times, especially when she runs off with one of my plant cuttings in her mouth."

He laughed. "She looks like she could be a lot of fun."

"She is." Amelia came into the kitchen and picked up Misty to cuddle her before setting her down by her food which she started to eat.

"I hope you don't mind, but I made a pot of coffee," he said as the maker stopped making the gurgling noise and the scent of the beans filled the air.

"Not at all," she said as she made her way over to pour the hot liquid into the cups he'd already put out. "Please, go sit at the table and I'll bring them over."

She was quite small compared to his height; her head was just below his shoulder. As she looked up at him, he could smell the scent of her shampoo. It reminded him of newly opened coconuts. For a moment Liam looked at her, trying to measure her expression, but she was hiding it well.

He did as he was asked and drew a chair out from beneath the pinewood table. Sitting down, he leaned back and folded his arms, watching her. He noticed a slight discomfort in her demeanor, as if she wasn't used to having people in her kitchen. Her face was pale and fatigued, and there was no doubt in his mind that there was something wrong.

Amelia placed their coffee on the table, then she went back to the counter and picked up a small, white, ceramic bowl with sugar cubes and a matching milk jug from the refrigerator.

Sitting down opposite him, she sipped her drink after doctoring it to her taste. "Please help yourself," she said, indicating with her hand.

"I like it black, but I have a sweet tooth." He took three lumps of sugar and dropped them in his coffee one at a time.

She smiled. "By all accounts, a very sweet tooth."

He stirred it and chuckled. It was good to see her smile.

A small silence followed, and although he was fine with it, she looked uncomfortable. He hesitated, measuring her a little. There was no doubt about her beauty, although he had a feeling she had no idea of her sensuality. Certainly, he could detect a degree of innocence.

"You're staring," she said, slightly breathless.

He grinned. "I find you very attractive," he said, never one to mince his words.

"Oh," she said nervously as she sipped her coffee. "Thank you." A faint flush tinged her cheeks.

"You're welcome."

She stirred uneasily in her chair, and he could see that she wasn't used to compliments. He couldn't understand that…she was gorgeous.

"I can see I'm making you feel uncomfortable, and I'm sorry about that." He frowned, because he hated the thought of making any woman feel like that. So, he decided for the moment to take things slow with her.

"How long have you lived here?" he asked.

"Cape Charles?"

He nodded.

"Four years."

"I get the feeling you don't like talking about

yourself."

"Really, whatever gave you that idea?" she exclaimed, cynicism doctoring her tone.

"Oh, probably the sarcasm and the one-word answers," he murmured.

She shrugged her shoulders.

"Let's change the subject a little. Why were you standing outside in the rain?"

Her hands cupped her mug of coffee, an apprehensive look in her eyes as if she didn't know what else to do with them. He regarded her for a minute. She was so tense, and as she looked away from him, she bit her lip nervously. She cleared her throat awkwardly before turning back to face him.

"I thought I saw Misty stuck in the tree," she finally said.

He narrowed his eyes. "Umm, not a very good liar, are you?" he replied with heavy irony.

By the look on her face, she was not amused by his frankness.

"I think it's time you left, Liam," Amelia said as she stood up.

He followed suit and tucked his chair back under the table.

"I'm sorry," he said. "It's none of my business."

"No, it isn't."

"Look," he said, deciding to be honest, "I like you, do you like me?"

She sighed. "I have no room in my life for a relationship." Her tone was despairing.

He followed her as she walked him to the door. She had her hand on the door handle when he covered it with his own. Amelia didn't move it, but she looked up at him.

He could drown in those eyes and die happy, but only after he'd helped her get rid of whatever sadness was buried inside her.

His mouth curved into a smile. "You have nothing to fear from me, Amelia. I would never hurt you."

Two deep lines of worry appeared between her eyes. "And what if it's the other way around? I could hurt you."

"I'm a big boy, why don't you let me make that decision for myself?" He took a deep breath. "How about dinner tonight at the Gingernut Pub?"

She lowered her thick, black lashes, as if she didn't want him to see what she was thinking, and he watched keenly as he waited for her answer.

She looked back up at him "Okay. Just dinner."

"Whatever you want," he said as he squeezed her hand before opening the door and letting it go.

Liam had been surprised by her answer, he'd expected her to say no. He felt as though he'd just chipped a tiny bit of her armor off, and it made him feel good, great actually…fan-fucking-tastic.

"I'll pick you up about seven. Does that work for you?" he asked.

She nodded. "Yes. See you then."

He walked down the path to his SUV and pressed the button to open the car door. Opening it, he climbed in and shut the door after him. He put the key in the ignition and started it, and the soft purr jumped to life. Liam reached for his seatbelt, put it on, and looked back at the house. There was no sign of her.

He'd always felt protective of those who had been bullied or needed help. He wasn't one to stand aside and just let bad things happen. Max had taught him to stick up for himself, and now he stood up for other people who needed it.

And he was pretty sure Amelia was in some sort of trouble. He could feel the vibes of fear even though she did a great job of hiding them.

Damn it.

He could have cut his tongue out after the look she'd given him when he'd complimented her. Most women loved them, but he'd already established that she was different. The truth was he couldn't wait to see her again.

Shit. What was happening to him?

His cell pinged, and he picked it up. It was a text message from Jarrod asking where he was.

Liam was beginning to think that his life was about to change a whole lot. The tug of attraction was there, and it had been a long time since someone had stirred his heart—a very long time.

****

Amelia had a raging headache and didn't want to think about anything; it hurt too much. So, after Liam left, she took some Advil from her bedside drawer. Picking up the glass of water from her bedside cabinet, she swallowed the pills. Amelia set the glass back down next to the book she was currently reading.

Drawing the covers back, she sat on the side of the bed. Slipping her tennis shoes off, Amelia lay on the cool sheets. She knew it was the only way to get the better of the migraine that was about to start.

What on earth had happened? Was she going crazy? Amelia turned on her side, putting her hands beneath her cheek, and frowned. She'd been so sure there had been someone behind that tree watching her, and what about that strange phone call?

In the back of her mind she was always aware of everything around her, especially if it felt strange. But she'd lived here for so long, and nothing had even come close to what she'd felt today. It was a gut instinct, a feeling in the pit of her stomach.

Laying on her back with a disgruntled sound, she blew her bangs from her face. Her throat tightened as she recalled that memorable look on Angus Rossi's face. But there was no way he was out of prison. He'd been sentenced to life imprisonment with the possibility of parole in twenty-five years, and it hadn't even been ten years yet. The misery of it still gave her nightmares.

Amelia had seen way too much, and witnessed too many painful scenes, which was one of the reasons she had this dull ache of foreboding inside her.

Was she just being silly? Amelia mentally kicked herself up the ass. *You're being ridiculous.* Tony could have hurt her years ago when they last met. However, blood was thicker than water, especially with the Rossi brothers, and perhaps things had happened that she knew nothing about.

Her head was pounding now. She needed to stop thinking about it, at least until her headache was gone. Closing her eyes, she thought about Liam, and a warm glow flowed through her, which was a little bit—no, it was *a lot* surprising.

Thoughts of him took away the shadows in her heart. He made her smile as she turned to her other side, facing the window.

She was fascinated by that sexy dimple on his chin. It had been so long since Amelia had found a man attractive that she almost forgot what it was like. The only sex she'd had since Tony was with a vibrator, which she hardly ever used now; it wasn't worth the trouble.

But Liam made her feel things she hadn't felt in forever. She wasn't sure if it was the tingling in her belly or the way his gaze unfolded when he looked at her. Amelia tried to curtail the electric current that was rampaging her body. It would be so easy to get lost in the way his eyes held her captive.

She felt breathless like an eighteen-year-old, and she was so caught up in her emotions for him that she didn't want it to blindside her. She could imagine going for a walk holding his hand, sitting on the porch with a glass of wine, or just hugging each other.

But she had to remind herself that none of those things would ever be possible. She couldn't stop the tear that fell down her cheek. First one then two, then sobs came from her until she was so exhausted her eyes shut and she slept.

Chapter 4

Liam drove down the street that led to Amelia's home. His large SUV growled as he slowed down to come to a stop outside her small house. He sat for a moment and took in the view of the Chesapeake Bay. It wasn't cold, but there was a mist settling over the still waters, and although it had been sunshine and showers all day, the temperature was around sixty-eight degrees at seven PM.

His mind wandered to the time when Max, Jarrod, and himself had made promises to each other that they would make something of their lives and that they wouldn't allow their circumstances to determine the outcome.

It had been hard studying and working, but the three of them had done good, and all that hard work had paid off. Jarrod owned his own company, and probably had more money than either Liam or Max. The eldest of the three, Max, worked for the government with his aero designs. And Liam hadn't done too badly either. He was good at what he did and loved it.

Liam had made partner at twenty-six, the youngest in DC at the time, and now he owned the law firm that gave him his first case. He remembered the days when he didn't have enough food to eat and holes in the soles of his shoes that he'd had to superglue. Yes, he'd done real good for a kid who'd had no parental guidance. The thought made him smile. He didn't flaunt his wealth, but knowing that his bank balance was very healthy gave him great satisfaction.

Now both Max and Jarrod were married with families, and Liam was the only bachelor left. In his experience real love was a myth…until his two friends had married, then he wasn't so sure, because when he looked at Max and Jarrod and how happy they were Liam floundered a little with his perceptions.

Shaking the thoughts from his head, he reached for the car keys and drew them out. Opening the door, he stepped out onto the road and used the button on his key fob to lock the door. Liam walked up the path to Amelia's front door and rang the bell.

The scent of vanilla filled his senses. The smell drifted from the baskets of flowers she had hanging on hooks on either side of her door. There was an array of shapes, all swaying in the gentle breeze, almost dancing with each other.

When Amelia opened the door, it was almost impossible to take his gaze from her and speak. She looked beautiful. A simple blue dress with a v-neck, just enough to display a small cleavage, her feminine, silky skin exposed. The material fitted to her narrow waist and then fell just slightly above her knee. Matching strappy sandals with slim heels set the outfit off beautifully.

She looked gorgeous and sexy as all hell. He had to swallow down the desire that shot through his body.

"Come in. I just need to get my purse," she said as she turned around.

He stepped inside the house. "You look lovely," he said.

"Thank you."

She picked up her purse and tucked it under her arm as she faced him. But the smile she gave him didn't reach her eyes. And come to think of it, she didn't look very well. Her eyes were narrowed as if it was painful to open them, and a grimace around her mouth told him that something wasn't right.

He walked forward until he was standing in front of her. "Are you okay?" he asked as he bent slightly to look into her eyes.

She nodded then groaned.

"What's wrong?" He laid his hand on her shoulder.

"It's fine, just a headache."

Obviously not just a normal headache. She was in real pain.

He took the purse from her and set it back on the table.

"What are you doing?" she asked in a surprised tone.

"Amelia, have you looked at yourself?"

"What are you talking about? Of course I did when I was dressing."

"No, I mean really looked."

"Have I got something on my face?" Amelia asked him with a hoarse whisper, and he could see she was getting a little annoyed by the way her lips pursed.

Liam sighed, but he remembered a time when his secretary had migraines and she looked the same way Amelia did now. That same parlor in her skin, her eyes heavy because of the light, and the pain in the depth of her pupils.

"If you've changed your mind about going out, that's fine," she said.

He almost laughed at her spirit, but he guessed that wouldn't go down well. Her breath was coming quickly, and with every breath, he caught a glimpse of two perfect, mouth-watering mounds of flesh where her nipples were outlined with the material of her dress.

When he looked back up at her face, she had gone bright red. Caught out, but he felt no shame. She was a beautiful woman. And at least she had some color now.

"I think it's time you left. Goodnight, Liam." She turned around and went to stand at the kitchen sink, not even looking at him.

Oh, fuck!

"Amelia, you have the wrong idea. I merely noticed that you weren't looking very well, and when you said you had a headache, I surmised that it was no ordinary headache." His tone was patient as he tried to redeem his actions.

Rotating to face him, she leveled him with an icy stare. Then she took a deep breath and softened her expression. She rubbed her hand over her face before shoving it into the pocket of her dress.

"I'm sorry," she said, her voice tight with pain. "And you're right, I do have a migraine." She kept her voice low and even, as if it hurt to talk. "I'm not usually so uptight."

"Look, I have a proposition for you." He moved nearer to her.

She regarded him with curiosity.

"I say we cancel our dinner out, and I cook for us instead. That way you can perhaps rest a little and see if you can get rid of that headache."

"You cook?"

He chuckled. "Don't sound so surprised. I was a student once—it was either cook or starve."

He tried to read her, but she was good at hiding her

thoughts, and at that moment he couldn't read them.

"I hardly know you," she murmured, her head slightly bowed.

There it was again, that hesitation in her voice. "No, you don't," he said with sincerity, trying to sound genuine. "But I promise that you can trust me."

Liam was normally good at reading people, but she was another story. This wasn't the first time he'd picked up vibes from her of someone who'd been hurt. Her eyes were pensive, as if she was trying to make a decision, and she pressed her fingers to her forehead.

Liam moved until he was standing in front of her. "Come on, baby girl. Let me help you."

A ghost of a smile briefly passed her lips before she grabbed hold of him, and if he hadn't been there, she would have dropped to the floor. He gathered her up in his arms, her slight weight nothing to him.

It was easy to find her room; he'd seen her go into it earlier.

He strode over to her bed and laid her down. Sitting on the edge, he pushed her hair back from her brow with his fingers. She didn't have a temperature, which was something.

At that moment her eyes opened, and for a split second, he could see on her face that she was unsure of what had happened. He saw immediately in her expression when she realized, and she took a deep, steadying breath.

"I'm so sorry, Liam."

"For what?"

"Passing out. Damn migraines."

"Don't be. It's always a pleasure when a woman collapses into my arms." He winked at her.

A smile flickered on her lips, but she suddenly went green around the gills and jumped from the bed, making a beeline for a door which she flung open.

He followed her into what was a bathroom. She was leaning over the toilet, heaving her insides out. He went to the sink, took a washcloth from the towel rail, and ran it under the cold tap. Going down on his haunches, he held her hair back until she kneeled back, bringing the lid down, and flushed the toilet.

When she turned to him he could see the horror in her eyes. Before she had a chance to say anything he drew the wet cloth across her forehead and cheeks.

"Finished?" he asked.

She nodded.

He slipped his arm around her and picked her up. Amelia lay her head on his chest. He didn't question the act; it just seemed the most natural thing to do.

She didn't fight him, just tucked her face into his neck. Her bed was only a few steps away, but as he carried her there he could feel her warm breath on his skin, and a mysterious emotion that he couldn't name enveloped him.

Liam lay her on the bed leaned down and removed her shoes, then he looked up at her and frowned.

"I'm sorry you had to see that," she said, scrubbing a hand over her face.

"I didn't have to. I could have walked away and left you, but I chose not to."

Drawing the throw that was on the bed over her, he smiled.

"Try and see if you can sleep that headache off, and I'll make us something to eat."

"I already slept this afternoon." She spoke with

fatigue in her voice. "And besides, there's no food in the house, nothing that you can make a meal with anyway."

"Why don't you let me worry about that?" he said sincerely, because he wanted to look after her. It was a crazy way to feel about a woman he hardly knew.

Taking the glass from her nightstand, he went to the bathroom and filled it with water. By the time he came back she was fast asleep. He looked at her glorious red hair spread out on the pillow. It was beautiful, and he imagined running his fingers through its silkiness.

Liam leaned down and tucked a curl behind her ear, smoothing the back of his hand over her cheek to check that she wasn't too hot. Her skin was velvety to the touch, and he acted as though it was the most natural thing to do.

Only it wasn't. He'd never looked after anyone else in his life. Well, he had, but not a woman. Max, Jarrod, and himself looked out for each other…but a woman? He shook his head and turned to go. Opening the door, he looked over his shoulder just to make sure she was still asleep.

He could feel himself sinking into a sensation he had no idea how to handle. Was this what his two friends had talked about when they got married?

Oh, fuck!

****

Amelia woke, somewhat confused for a moment as to where she was. Then she remembered how she had gotten there, and she groaned. When she looked toward her window, it was pitch-black, but a lamp had been switched on by her bed so the light was low and not bright.

Sitting up, she reached for the glass of water beside

her and sipped at the liquid before swinging her legs to the floor. Her head hurt, but not as much as it had. She sat for a moment and realized it was a bearable pain. Then something caught her eye, and she looked beyond the dressing table to see Liam fast asleep in her bamboo chair.

His long body was stretched out, eyes closed, and arms folded over his chest. It appeared he'd changed clothes. When he'd come to pick her up he'd had slacks on, but now he wore blue jeans with a black t-shirt which had shifted slightly up his body, exposing a flat belly with a smattering of hair dipping below his waistband.

Her heart nearly missed a beat. Liam seemed to have that effect on her.

She couldn't help but stare at him. She hadn't had a man in her bedroom for a long time, and never in this one. The air in the room was cool against her warm skin. She sincerely doubted that any woman would not feel attracted to this man.

Amelia was desperate for the bathroom. She didn't want to stop looking at him, but needs must, and she slid off the bed and padded across the carpet to the bathroom. Shutting the door, she used the facilities. After washing her hands, she quietly opened the door.

"How are you feeling?" Liam asked.

She looked over at him, and he held her gaze, waiting for her to speak.

"Much better, thank you. I'm sorry that I spoilt your evening." She drew her hands up and down the sides of her dress, a little anxious as she sought to erect that wall of defense she was so good at activating when needed.

Liam tilted his head and smiled as if he knew what she was trying to do. Amelia looked away and stood there like an idiot, unsure of what to do next. Jeez, how old was she? She was acting like a teenager who had snuck a boy into her room. Setting her shoulders back, she faced him.

"Thank you for staying. But I'm sure you'll want to be going now," she said with her sternest voice. "You must be exhausted."

Liam looked at her with a nonchalant smile as he stood up and stretched his hands above him, yawning and growling out a roar of pleasure. Her gaze automatically moved down his body as he flexed every muscle, drawing her eyes to the low rise of his jeans' waistband.

Heat pooled in her belly, making her fingertips tingle. *Oh, dear Lord!*

He looked at his watch. "It's three-thirty in the morning. How about a coffee before I go? I made you a chicken salad. It's wrapped in the fridge." An irresistible smile and warmth echoed in his voice.

Damn, it was the least she could do.

"Have you eaten?" she asked him as she opened the bedroom door.

"Yeah. Sorry, I was starving."

"Don't apologize." She turned to him. "Thank you for making me some food."

He nodded, and she went to the kitchen and took two cups from the drainer where they had been left to dry.

"Would you mind if I asked you something?" Liam said.

With a deliberately casual movement, she turned to face him and folded her arms in front of her. He was leaning one shoulder against the doorframe, his hands half-pushed into his jeans pockets.

"Depends what it is," she said a little warily.

"What are you afraid of?" he asked with no expression at all on his face.

The fact of the matter was that she couldn't tell him, not ever. How could she tell him that she was in hiding from a man who wouldn't think twice about killing him to get to her?

Amelia chewed at her bottom lip and was saved from answering at that instant by the beep of the coffee maker he'd turned on a moment ago. Pouring the liquid into the cups, she brought them over to the countertop opposite her and set them down.

She pulled out one of the swivel stools and sat on it. Amelia couldn't avoid his question forever. She could tell that he wasn't the type of person to let her get away with not answering.

"Afraid? I don't know what you're talking about."

"Amelia," he said as he took a few steps to the counter and sat opposite her.

She cocked her head to one side and raised her eyebrows.

"How long are we going to pussyfoot around this? I knew the moment I met you that something wasn't right, and now I see it even more."

Jeez, were her expressions that easy to read? She was normally good at hiding her feelings. The cornflower blue of his eyes looked deeper than normal, and she looked away from them, because they were like a lie radar. She had never felt comfortable lying even though her life was a necessary deception, a deviation from the truth.

Amelia saw concern on his face, and she couldn't remember the last time a man had shown her that. She nervously tapped her fingers against the cool surface, until she saw him glance at her hands. She stopped, and to have something to do with her hands, she picked up her coffee cup and sipped the hot drink.

"Why don't we talk about you?" she said, hoping to defer his prying eyes from what she had hidden for so long.

"Okay, I'll buy it, but eventually you'll talk to me. And until then there is nothing I can do to help you."

Help her? He would never be able to do that; no one could.

"Did you grow up in DC?" she asked.

"Kinda," he said, leaning forward onto his forearms and clasping his hands together.

And he told her about his childhood. Funnily enough, their childhoods were strangely similar, except he'd made two good friends whereas she had no one.

"I guess you could call yourself the three musketeers," she said with a smile.

His smile broadened. "The candy bar or the actual fighting threesome?" he said with a glint of humor.

Amelia brought up her hand to stifle her giggles. "Silly man, the three men with swords and camaraderie," she managed through her joviality.

"Well, I don't know about swords, but we've certainly been through a few dynamic actions in our times together."

Judging by his expression, she could tell that he held a great deal of affection for his two friends.

"Tell me about Jarrod and Max," Amelia requested. She was glad that the conversation had been successfully steered away from her.

"Jarrod you've met in the coffee shop?"

She nodded, remembering when they'd walked in.

Both were tall and handsome and had a commanding presence without even knowing it.

"He's married to Maisy, and they have three dogs and a newly arrived baby named Mia, who is adorable."

He smiled, and it was clear to her that Mia was special to him by the way his tone changed in his voice, all soft and delicate.

"Max is married to a girl from the UK, and she looks after her nephew, and the three of them seem to be very happy."

"So, you're the bachelor of the group."

He nodded as a devilish look came into his eyes. "I'm enjoying life too much to settle down."

Somehow she got the feeling that he wasn't being altogether honest, which struck her as odd. Why would he lie about it?

"What about you?" he asked. "Boyfriend? Someone to keep you warm at night?"

"I can assure you, I do not need a man to keep me warm any time, and besides," she said, flashing him a teasing smile, "I have a very good electric blanket for that."

He laughed loudly and leaned more forward so that he was within inches of her face. She could see every line, the laughter lines that splayed out at the sides of his nice eyes, the five-o'clock shadow that grazed his skin, and that dimple on his chin.

She lifted her gaze and looked into his eyes. They were so damned sexy that she couldn't even bring herself to look away. She felt light-headed, and her breath was slightly irregular. Studying his face made her heart pound a little against her ribs, and the prolonged anticipation was almost unbearable.

"But it's not going to make you feel like you're the most beautiful woman in the world or tell you that your skin is like silk or nibble your ear and whisper sweet nothings."

Holy cow!

Her heart lurched madly, and she couldn't tear her gaze away from those lips, even when he'd finished talking.

"Amelia?"

She tingled when he said her name. "Yes?"

His fingers lifted her chin so that she was looking him straight in the eye.

"I want to kiss you. May I?"

Oh, good Lord, he was asking, and that melted her heart. She couldn't formulate any words, so she just nodded her agreement.

His tongue traced the fullness of her lips before they covered hers. Liam was surprisingly gentle. He was slow and thoughtful, and it sent shivers of desire down her spine. It didn't take her long to return the kiss, although she was surprised she remembered how to. One thing was for sure—this man knew how to make her feel good.

****

Liam enjoyed the tenderness of her touch. She was almost shy, definitely not experienced, and a little hesitant, but she tasted just as good as he thought she would. He hadn't had such an explosive reaction to a woman in a long time…if ever.

"Liam." Her voice was a whisper, but he barely heard her over the drumming of his heartbeat. There was a throbbing silence for a mere second before he opened his mouth on hers, insatiably ravenous.

They were still opposite each other with the counter

between them, and he wanted to touch her, hold her, but he didn't want to stop. His tongue touched hers, and it was like a lightning shock through his body. He could feel the hairs on his arms stand up like spikes.

Amelia was tentative at first, but it wasn't long before she was sliding her tongue along his and kissing him with such lust he felt sure he wasn't going to survive. He reached for her hands that were laying on the countertop and laced his fingers through hers, her short nails digging into his skin.

There were sounds of pleasure coming from her throat, and damn if that didn't make him feel even hotter than he was already. Jesus, he was on fire! His erection was painful against the zipper of his pants, and his breathing was erratic.

Through the muffled sounds of their liaison, he heard the cat door open and shut. Liam pulled away from her and looked around. He could smell smoke. Amelia must have as well, because she turned away from him, and then she screamed. His body went rigid as he followed her gaze. Someone had rolled a bottle filled with liquid across the floor, and it was on fire. Fuck! It was a petrol bomb.

He hauled Amelia across the top of the counter and tackled her to the ground, covering her body with his. She screamed just before there was an explosion. Fragments of glass rained down on them. He took the brunt of the blast and felt bits of fire falling on top of him. He had completely covered Amelia's body to protect her.

He sat up and looked down at her white face.

"Are you okay?" he asked.

"Yes," she whispered. "What the hell was that?" she

exclaimed. "Shit, you're on fire." She reached up to pull the tablecloth off the table and used it to pat out the flame. "Are you all right?"

He nodded and cupped her cheek as she sat upright and he went into a crouched position.

James took hold of her hand and stood. "Come on, we need to get out of here."

"Misty?" she asked panicked.

"She went out," Liam said as he pulled her up to her feet gripping her hand as he made his way out of the kitchen. There was no door; it had been completely blown off its hinges. They went out into the garden, coughing and breathing in the fresh air.

He saw her swallow. She had bits of glass in her hair, and he picked them out.

"Baby, are you sure you're not hurt?" he asked again, his eyes smarting from the smoke.

"No…just shocked." The words tumbled from her mouth.

"Milly, are you all right?"

They both looked to where the voice was coming from. It was an older woman. She walked toward them, looking concerned.

"Yes, Mrs. Jameson. Stand back from the house, just in case."

"I've called the sheriff and the fire department."

Amelia reached for the woman's hand and pulled her away from the house. The three of them went and stood in Mrs. Jameson's small front yard.

"God, Milly, what happened?" the neighbor asked her.

"I don't know, Mrs. Jameson."

Liam was glad she didn't tell the woman. There was

no sense in putting the fear of God into the old woman.

"It was a massive bang. I heard it in my bedroom."

Amelia looked down at the woman's clothing and frowned. Obviously, she had just realized that her neighbor was wearing her night clothes. "Goodness, Mrs. Jameson, you're going to catch a chill." She pulled the woman to her side. "Let's get you inside." They both guided her to her front door.

"Are you sure you're okay? Do you need somewhere to stay?"

Before she could answer, Liam spoke. "No, she'll be fine, Mrs. Jameson. I'll look after her."

The neighbor's eyes were full of apprehension as she looked over at Amelia, and Liam knew the woman was uncertain of what to do.

"Would you like to come inside while you wait? It's cold out here."

"No, thank you. We're fine." Amelia put her hand on Mrs. Jameson's. "Don't worry, I'll be okay."

The woman frowned a moment, and then nodded as she shut her door. Amelia stood next to Liam as they waited for the emergency services to arrive.

"Are you sure you're okay?" she asked him, looking up at his face. "God, what if that explosion had hit you? What the hell was it? I don't understand."

"Stop." The single word was a bit harshly said, but he didn't want her to go down that route.

"What?" Her voice trembled as she looked up at him.

"Don't play the 'what if' words in your mind. We're okay. No one was hurt, and that's the main thing."

He drew her closer to his side. Why would someone do that to her? It was clearly meant to harm or even kill her. A cold shudder went through him. He couldn't help but be thankful that he had still been at her house.

The sound of sirens could be heard coming down the street. A fire engine pulled up to her house, and a fireman jumped out and came toward them.

"In the kitchen at the back of the house," Liam said, pointing the way.

The fireman nodded and shouted at someone to bring a hose.

The sheriff's vehicle, its blue lights flashing, pulled up and parked next to the fire engine. An officer climbed out of the SUV and put his hat on before closing the door and coming toward them.

He was a big guy, and he walked with purposeful strides until he stopped in front of where they were standing and tipped his hat. "I'm Sheriff Seth Tayside. Is this your property?" he asked, looking at Liam.

"It's mine," Amelia murmured.

Liam could tell that she might be in shock, and he was keeping a close eye on her.

"Are you hurt, ma'am?" the sheriff asked Amelia.

She shook her head in reply.

"I'm her friend, Liam Miller. I was here when the incident happened."

"Okay, so would you like to explain what occurred?"

"Yeah, sure," he said and recapped for the sheriff everything that had happened.

The sheriff looked over at Amelia and asked, "Is that information correct, ma'am?"

She nodded.

"Are there any additional details you'd like to add?"

She shook her head. "No," she said quietly.

"Okay. I want to take a look around, but if you wouldn't mind meeting me at the office so I can take down your statements. I realize it's four-thirty AM," he said, looking at his watch. "But it's best to do it now while it's clear in your minds."

"Of course," Liam said, taking hold of Amelia's arm.

"Do you need a ride to the station?" the sheriff asked.

"No, I have my car," Liam answered.

He led Amelia to his vehicle. He unlocked the passenger side door for her, and she climbed in, almost as if she were on automatic pilot. He rounded the hood and opened his door, getting in. He leaned his forearms on the steering wheel and looked at her.

"You okay?" He drew his brows together, looking at her uncertainly.

She smiled smoothly, betraying nothing of what had just happened. It was a bleak, tight-lipped smile. "Yes, I'm fine, thanks."

Clasped hands lay on top of her lap, the dress showing smoke colorings and little spots where the burning shards had melted the material. God, they'd been lucky to get out of there alive. He was fairly certain that she had been targeted. No way was it kids…it had been meant for Amelia, and what he wanted to know was why.

****

With all the commotion going on, no one realized they were being watched from the shadows. It couldn't have gone any better. Amelia looked terrified. It was going to be so much fun. She would pay for every single minute of the agony that had entered their lives.

It was all in the preparation, and this had been a long

time coming. It had taken years to finally find her, and it was going to be fun watching her suffer. Although it was obvious that her 'man friend' was very protective of her, which would make it a little harder to get closer.

But nothing would stop the plan. Amelia would suffer in the end; it didn't matter what she did or who was with her. It would not be an issue to kill Amelia's 'friend' too.

Tomorrow the next step to the plan would begin or end, depending on what happened. It was not a problem now, it was just a matter of following the signal.

The bitch was going to die.

Chapter 5

As Amelia sat in the sheriff's office she was almost
certain that what had just happened was not a random act
of violence. How did he find her, and why was he out of
prison?

She knew in her heart that it was her past catching
up with her. It had been inevitable, and she had become
complacent with everything. All she'd wanted was a
normal life, but she had been an idiot to think that was
ever going to happen. It was hard to accept the dull ache
of foreboding. The misery she was feeling was like a
steel weight against her chest.

Fury almost choked her. How dare Angus Rossi do
this to her? But did she really know it was him or one of
his gang? God, it had to be. Why would anyone else want
to do such a thing to her? She felt her shoulders droop,
and it was a sensation she hated.

Amelia looked up and saw Liam through the open
blinds of the office window, talking to the sheriff. Seth
Tayside was a big man, but she felt no fear when she was
around him. He'd been kind and patient. He'd asked her
questions that she had no answer to.

They'd both given statements, but she was keeping
a secret that none of them knew about. She pulled the
cover around her that Liam had taken from the back of
his SUV when she had been shivering.

There was a buzz of continuous movement in this

small room, not like when she had been in the UK and being cared for by detectives in one of the largest police offices in the world, Scotland Yard.

"Here you go, honey," said a woman who was rotund in stature but had the most amazingly kind smile.

Amelia took the cup of coffee and smiled back. "Thank you."

"No problem. If you need anything else, my name is Elsie, and I'm over at that desk." She pointed to an empty chair.

"You're very kind," Amelia said.

"Not at all, honey." The nice lady patted her on the shoulder before returning to her area.

Amelia sipped the steaming liquid. She thought it was coffee, but it was tea, a sweet infusion. A few moments later she saw Liam heading toward her. She put the cup down on the desk beside her and stood up, drawing the cover that had slipped down her shoulders.

"Can we go now?" she asked him, comforted by the sight of this man whom she hardly knew.

He nodded. "Yes, we can leave."

It was going to be hard to leave this place that she'd considered her home. But surprisingly, Amelia found that it would be harder to leave behind what could have been a very nice relationship with a man that she had truly begun to like.

"Did the sheriff say anything about what has happened?" There was an element of hope in her voice, but she knew the answer before Liam opened his mouth.

"I'm sorry, but there are no leads. Nothing like this has ever happened in Cape Charles, so it seems really odd to me, almost as if you were targeted." Liam was looking at her as if trying to gauge her thoughts.

"Well, that's just silly. Who would want to do that to me?"

"That's exactly what the sheriff said. Come on," he said, placing his arm around her.

She was shocked for a moment and was about to step out of his hold when he squeezed her tighter as if knowing what she was going to do. And it did feel good.

Once they were in his car and driving toward her home she looked over at him and said, "Thank you for staying with me. It was very kind of you."

He frowned at her. "Did you honestly think that I would just walk away?" He gave her a sidelong glance of utter disbelief.

She shrugged. "I wouldn't have blamed you."

"Seems you have been mixing with the wrong people if you think I would do that."

He didn't realize how true that had been. She had gotten involved with the wrong people, and was paying for it. Now she was worried about him, and anyone else who knew her.

A wave of apprehension swept through her as they stopped outside her house. To look at the front, it was as if nothing had happened. However, she knew that just taking a single step inside would change that perception.

By the time she thought about getting out, Liam was already opening her door.

"Pack some things that you think you might need for a few days."

"Where am I going?"

"Back to where I'm staying. I've already cleared it with the hotel."

"But I don't need to leave. It's only the kitchen that's a mess."

"A mess," he repeated with a tone that was quite clearly a little sarcastic, which got her back up.

"Mess or not, this is my home, and if you think that I'm just going to pack a bag and do as you say, you are very mistaken."

She jumped out of the car and misjudged how high it was. Her foot caught on the step, and she would have fallen had he not reached out and grabbed hold of her waist with his big hands.

"Oomph," she said as her feet touched the ground.

"You okay?" he asked.

"Yes…thank you," she said. "You saved me from falling flat on my face. Seems you're always saving me from something."

Their eyes met, and she felt a shock sizzle down her spine, tingling every nerve ending. For a second, they just stood there. She was tongue-tied—*how ridiculous*—and even more so when she saw the teasing expression on his face. She pushed him away and made her way to the front door. Taking her keys out of her pocket, she opened the door. As she stepped inside, the smell of smoke was prevalent, and she put her hand to her chest as she breathed in; it was almost painful..

She could see that the back door had been replaced. In the two hours that they had been at the sheriff's office, someone had fitted a new door where the other one had been blown away.

"Do you know who replaced the door?" she asked Liam, pointing to what had been an empty space. She needed to thank whoever it was.

"I called my friend, Jarrod. Luckily, he had a spare one that he made to fit."

"Oh," she said, surprised again by this man. "Thank

you. Can you ask him to send me the bill?"

"Don't worry about it. Jarrod didn't mind at all."

"No, I want to pay him."

"Oh, for goodness sake, Amelia, stop doing that."

"What?" she exclaimed.

"Pushing people away when they want to help."

She drew her hands over her face and then through her hair. She didn't want to have this conversation now. She was too exhausted.

As she looked around the kitchen, her heart dropped to her feet. The mess was so much worse than she had anticipated. There was nothing left. It was as if the room was gutted, and the vile stench of smoke was almost too much to bear.

She had to leave. There was no way in hell she could stay in Cape Charles now. But where was she going to go? She had no idea, but that never stopped her before. She would just get on a bus and see where it took her. As long as she could hide herself again.

Oh God, the whole thing was going to start all over again. Being on the run! Would she ever be free?

Amelia turned to look at Liam. *I will not break down. I will not break down.* She silently repeated the mantra, trying to muster up enough energy to tell him to go.

"I've been looking after myself for a long time. I don't need you to feel responsible for me. The attack was just some silly kids, and I'm perfectly capable of taking care of myself."

"Amelia, I know you can look after yourself, but let me help? I want to."

She swallowed hard and lifted her gaze, which had been resting on the dimple on his chin, and met his gaze.

"Liam, I can't do this, not right now." Her brain struggled to find the right words. "I'm not ready for anything that has *us* in the title."

Pivoting away from him, she stepped over the mess and made her way out of the kitchen. That was the end of that—finished before it had started. This was her life. She knew it had been but a dream to even think she could have anything remotely normal.

****

Liam sighed, pushing his fingers through his hair with frustration as he watched her walk away from him. He was not about to leave her on her own—not even for one second—until it was exactly clear to him what was going on…if anything.

This type of attack had never happened in this small community. The sheriff had said there had been no other occurrences in the area. It had been a long night. Looking at his watch, he saw that it was a 7:15 AM.

Liam had given the sheriff his cell number, just in case anything popped up. He had hoped it might have been a chance act of violence, but in his mind he knew that it was something different. It was just too severe for something around here. Even where he lived in DC it would have been rare.

It had surprised him at how shaky he'd felt, but it wasn't every day that one was exposed to a situation like this. He'd told her she was staying with him, although he didn't normally act so neanderthal, but he was so concerned about her that he felt his choice was very limited.

When some asshole had tried to kill them both with a homemade bomb he didn't mind admitting that he nearly sprouted a full head of gray hairs. The reality of what had happened was settling in, and he was worried as hell about Amelia and what she was hiding.

He followed her upstairs and sat in the chair that he had spent half the night in. He could hear the shower running, and he waited patiently for her to come out. She stepped out of the bathroom, banging the door closed behind her.

She was wearing jeans and a t-shirt, and she appeared fresher than he felt or looked. Now that her face was clean of smoke he could see that she was pale and had dark rings beneath her eyes, and an ache squeezed at his heart.

He could see that trying to help Amelia was going to be an uphill battle, but it was one he was willing to fight.

"Do you make a habit of just coming into a woman's bedroom without being asked?"

"Never."

She stood there with a towel around her hair and her hands on her hips. Ah...a little bit of spirit was appearing. He smiled inwardly, being careful not to let her see.

"So, if you please...get out." She shook her wet hair free from the towel and scrunched it with her fingers. The thick, wavy tendrils hung loosely over her shoulders and down her back.

When she saw him looking at her a heightened color spread across her cheeks. Amelia's chest heaved with her breathing, and it took his eyes on a journey of pure nirvana as his gaze focused on the nipples that were poking through the material of her t-shirt. Following the line down, her body was slender but curvaceous.

Tight jeans clung to shapely thighs and calves. Her

feet were bare and her toenails painted a dark pink. It was a few seconds before he looked back up at her face. She was exquisite, but what was more interesting to him was that she had no idea of her beauty.

As she went to stand by the door he could see the determination in her expression that she wanted him gone. "Time you left," she said.

"No can do," he replied.

"I'll call the sheriff." She gave him a hostile glare.

"By all means do," he said, taking his cell phone out of his pocket and offering it to her.

"Bloody hell, will you just leave me alone?" she blurted out.

He almost laughed when she cursed at him. She turned away to go stand by the window. Her shoulders were slumped as she wrapped her arms around herself.

"Hey." He leaned forward with his elbows on his knees and hands clasped together. His tone was gentle as he tried to choose his words carefully. "Why don't you pack a few things and come back to my room for today and tonight, which will give you time to make some calls, get a good night's sleep, and sort out anything else? And if you feel like you need to return tomorrow, then I won't stop you."

For a moment there was silence, but then she nodded. "Okay," she murmured and turned back to face him. "Just one night."

"Pack a bag then. I'll go downstairs and wait for you."

"Mrs. Jameson texted me that she had managed to persuade Misty to go indoors. I want to go by Mrs. Jameson's house and check on her. And I need to ask if she'll keep Misty for me."

He nodded. "Don't worry if she won't—we'll sort something out." He eased into a smile before getting up and leaving her to pack.

Liam waited outside, sitting on one of the patio chairs as he answered some emails on his cell. It wasn't long before Amelia stepped out of the door, shutting it behind her and locking it.

"Here, I'll take that," he said, taking her small bag. "You go see Mrs. Jameson."

"Thank you." She gave him a polite smile.

Liam went to his car, flicking the button to unlock his vehicle. He set her bag on the back seat before opening the driver's side door and climbing in. Setting the rearview mirror so that he could see Amelia talking to her neighbor, he watched while she took hold of Misty and cuddled her before handing her back. She spoke for a few seconds more before waving goodbye and making her way toward him.

Her door opened and she pulled herself onto the seat. She fastened her seatbelt and then sat with her hands clasped in her lap.

"Everything okay?" he asked.

"No, but it soon will be," she said.

He had no idea what she meant, but now was not the time to question her.

****

Amelia sat in the chair in Liam's hotel room, which was more like a studio apartment. It had a small kitchen and of course its own bathroom, which wasn't always the case in the UK. She had her feet tucked beneath her as she tried to process the last twelve hours. She had the feeling in the pit of her stomach that she wanted to throw up, and she swallowed, trying to hold it back. There was no doubt in her mind that her past had come back to haunt her. Now she had to decide what to do.

She would have to go back to her house and pick up the backpack that she kept hidden. It hadn't been opened for four years, but it contained everything she needed for a quick getaway. All she had to do now was sneak out without Liam noticing.

She looked over at where he sat on the end of the bed talking to Lizzie for her. She hadn't felt like speaking to anyone, but she couldn't just not show up for work. By now everyone she knew would be aware of what had happened.

His voice was quiet and calm as he looked out of the window, his long legs stretched out in front of him. She couldn't understand why he was being so nice to her. A manic assault in her home could have killed him. It would have sent most men running…but not him.

The man she had sent to prison was a violent, nasty piece of work. If only she hadn't been so naïve about her relationship with Tony. He'd made her feel special, and for a girl like her, who had nothing, it had felt amazing when Tony paid attention to her.

The first time she had seen Tony she had been serving behind the kiosk of a petrol station. Her eyes had immediately been drawn to the red Audi sports car, and especially the handsome man that got out to fill his car with fuel. And that was the start of her relationship with Tony Rossi.

Liam finally put the phone down on the bed after making a few more calls. She hadn't been listening, but now she watched as he rubbed his hand over his short hair, a slight agitation showing in his eyes.

"Lizzie wanted to come and see you, but I said you

were sleeping. Was that okay?"

She nodded. "Yes, thanks. I don't really feel up to facing anyone at the moment."

"I didn't think you would."

Amelia smiled. "Thank you."

"For what?" His dark brows slanted in a frown.

"For taking care of everything."

The fearful images of what could have happened were at the forefront of her mind. She had to take control, had to stop Liam from making any more of her decisions. However, she knew that he would be hard to shake off.

It would be so easy to just sit back and hide behind him. But that would be self-centered...so, so selfish.

She'd lived for years in a state of fear, and when she was finally learning to let go she'd been caught out. Which just went to show that she would never be able to stop looking over her shoulder.

Liam looked at her with an intense stare. It seemed as if he was trying to see past that wall of secrecy she had brought up to hide how she was feeling. But she was very good at hiding her emotions and fears.

Amelia could see that he was thinking, the cognitive wheels turning in his mind.

"Why don't you have a nap, and catch up on some sleep?" His voice had an infinitely compassionate tone. He sat at the desk and opened his laptop.

"It was probably just some kids messing around," she muttered. She knew in her heart that wasn't true, but she'd like to convince Liam it was.

He turned his head and pinned her with a stare. "Perhaps," he said with quiet emphasis. "But I think both you and I know that to be highly unlikely." His eyes narrowed slightly. "Unless you want to tell me something?"

Amelia knew in that moment that he sensed there was something else going on, and she watched as he rubbed his five-o'clock shadow, waiting for her to answer. The sun streamed through the window where he was sitting.

The scent of the peonies in the window box was sweet and reminded her of her own back garden. Guilt flooded her, and for a moment she almost gave in and told him what she thought was happening. But it was the thought of him being hurt that stopped her. She couldn't risk that.

"No," she said as convincingly as she could. "Nothing is going on that I know," she remarked in a clear, cool, and what she hoped was honest voice.

But based on the look of total disbelief in his eyes, it was obvious that she had failed miserably. He sighed and turned back to his laptop, immediately typing at the keys.

"What are you doing?" she asked him.

"Just thought I'd catch up on some work," he replied, his gaze still glued to the computer.

"Oh, okay."

She got up from her seat and went to the kitchen. There was a small coffee pot and kettle, with two cups and condiments beside it. She set about making a pot of coffee for Liam and put the kettle on for a cup of the camomile tea that was in the selection of tea bags.

Popping the bag in one of the cups, she leaned her back against the small worktop and folded her arms. How was she going to get away from Liam? Not that she particularly wanted to, but it was for his own safety.

She had to leave. It was a sad decision to make

because she had grown to love it here in this town that had become her home. And for some unusual reason that she couldn't answer, Amelia liked Liam. It was one of those things where there was no rhyme or reason. She couldn't explain why she felt that way.

Perhaps she could sneak out later when it was nighttime? Amelia felt as though her emotions were on a roller coaster and she couldn't find the brakes to stop them from crashing at the end of the line.

Once the coffee was brewed she poured him a cup and emptied some hot water into her mug. Carrying the drinks into the other room, she set the cup on the table beside his laptop.

He looked up at her. "You made coffee. How did you know it's exactly what I needed? Thank you," he said as he lifted the cup to his lips and closed his eyes. "This is definitely hitting the spot." He smiled at her.

Amelia glanced at the computer screen and was surprised to see the *Cape Charles Mirror*, which was their local newspaper.

"Did you find anything interesting?" she asked, looking back at him.

His smile suddenly vanished as if he was reminded of what he was doing.

"No, which is a good thing, but it doesn't explain what happened to you."

So, he'd been searching for any other incidents. She took a sip of her tea. He wouldn't find anything, because it had nothing to do with any local crime.

"Are you sure there is nothing you need to tell me, Amelia?"

Her stomach knotted, and Amelia tried to look completely innocent as she watched him, but she couldn't hold his stare, and she bit her lip, looking away. It would be so nice to share her problem with someone, but it was way too dangerous.

"No. Why would I? You know as much as I do."

His expression was grim, and an inner torment gnawed inside her, but instead of coming clean she looked past him to the bed. "Do you mind if I take a nap? Unless you need me for something?" She could see from the clock on the wall that it was ten minutes past noon. A few hours of closing her mind to everything was what she needed.

"Absolutely not. Go for it." His gaze was as soft as a caress. He was disturbing to her in more ways than one.

Without saying another word, she headed over to the bed and set her cup on the bedside table. Drawing back the covers, she lay down and pulled them over her. Sleep was the only thing that was going to help her.

****

Liam waited until Amelia was asleep before he got ready to go out. Going over to the side of the bed, he pulled the covers further up. She had a chin of iron determination, generously curved lips, and a small, pretty nose. The rich, glowing auburn of her glossy locks shone like lustrous glass and was spread over his pillows. He loved the look of her in his bed. He gently moved her bangs back from her forehead and used his thumb to smooth the skin.

She looked more peaceful, less worried. He wished she would trust him. Something was going on, but he didn't know what. He'd searched the local paper to see if anyone else had been targeted. But there was nothing. The crime rate in Cape Charles was almost nonexistent. He was totally perplexed as to what was happening in her life.

He walked over to the desk and scribbled a note saying he'd be back in a couple of hours. Perhaps Jarrod might be able to suggest a few things. Liam had asked a private detective he used to do a search and see if he could find anything associated with Amelia. He hated to do that, but he really wanted to get a handle on what on earth was turning her world upside down.

Shutting the door quietly behind him, Liam went into the elevator and pressed the button for the ground floor. As he stepped out into the warm sunshine, he took his sunglasses from his top pocket and slipped them on. He decided to walk. It had been a long night, and the fresh air would be good for him.

****

The hotel parking lot where the stranger had parked his SUV was quiet. Although the man had exited the hotel, there was no sign of Amelia.

Patience was a virtue.

The fact of the matter was that it was irrelevant who got hurt in the process. Amelia was the primary subject. To eliminate her was the priority.

Bombs were messy, but the thought of the disaster that it would inflict gave a shiver of anticipation. YouTube had been very explanatory on how to make one.

The difficult part had been getting all the supplies to make a bomb. But after discovering that a train going to the Appalachian Mountains was carrying the necessary supplies, it was simple enough to break into it.

The thrill would be watching it explode later. It had been easier than anticipated to get to the SUV in question. Opening the passenger door, the small torch gave enough light to work quickly even with the rain that had just started.

Deft fingers linked all the wires to an old mobile phone, and with hands that were shaking—not with fear, but excitement—the detonators were set into place. When the job was done and all connected, it had been a simple matter to crawl out from beneath the car and get a safe distance away from it. It would be such a pleasure to watch her burn all the way to hell.

****

Liam quietly opened the door to his hotel room. After spending a few hours with Jarrod and speaking to his detective he returned to find Amelia still asleep. She was on her back with both arms above her head. He could see the outline of her legs beneath the covers. She was sprawled out, almost taking up the whole bed.

He looked at his watch. It was four-thirty. The weather had changed dramatically since he first went out this morning, and it was now raining heavily. Geoff had dropped him off on his way home, but even just going from the car to the hotel door had been enough to soak him.

The rain was pounding at the open window, and he walked over and shut it before taking some clean clothes from the drawer and heading to the bathroom for a hot shower. Once he'd finished and was dressed in some dry clothes he went about setting the coffee pot on in the kitchen and then returned to the bedroom, his bare feet silent across the carpet.

Amelia was still out of it. It was time to wake her. Otherwise, she wouldn't be able to sleep tonight. Liam sat on the side of the bed and gently shook her. It took a moment before she opened her eyes, looking vaguely confused.

"Hey, sleepyhead."

She glanced around the room before focusing back on him. "What time is it?"

"Nearly five."

"At night?"

He nodded.

"Good Lord, I've been asleep for hours?" she asked with disbelief in her voice.

He smiled. "You missed lunch. In fact, you haven't eaten anything since yesterday."

"Do I smell coffee?" she asked, rubbing her eyes with her fingers.

"Yes. Stay where you are, and I'll bring you a cup."

When he came back she was sitting up in bed. As he approached she broke into a wide smile, and his pulse quickened. There was something about her that he most definitely appreciated.

Liam handed the mug to her. He was amused by her appreciation of the scent, and that was before she took a sip and moaned.

Well hell, that made him as hard as he could be beneath the zipper of his jeans. Thank goodness he hadn't tucked his t-shirt in.

"I can't believe I slept for so long," she said, yawning behind her hand.

"You must have needed it."

She shrugged.

"Thought we might go out for some food. You must be starving."

Just then her stomach made a growling noise, and she giggled.

"Oops, I think you may be right," she said,

swallowing back the last of the coffee. "I wouldn't mind a shower and a change of clothes." She drew back the covers as he stepped aside for her to get out of bed. "I feel downright scruffy."

She stood and stretched, and his eyes were instantly drawn to her nipples beneath her shirt. Hell, to him she looked far from scruffy.

Color washed over her cheeks as she saw him looking, and she wrapped her arms around herself. He hated that he'd made her feel uncomfortable. They stared at each other for a moment, the atmosphere taut with electricity, and then Amelia looked away from him.

Damn, he didn't want her to feel like that with him.

"Go and have a hot shower. I'll pour you another coffee. We'll take the car. It's a little wet out there."

She looked toward the window and nodded in agreement with him.

Liam turned toward the window. Was that thunder? Amelia must have heard it as well, because she tensed a little, and he could see her shoulders go rigid.

They both went to have a look, and in the parking lot below, fire and smoke were billowing up toward them.

"Someone has just blown my car up," he said almost matter-of-factly. "Get back from the window." Taking her elbow, he pulled her back several steps.

"What the hell?" she asked, looking at him.

"My thoughts exactly," Liam said, taking his cellphone from his pocket.

Chapter 6

Amelia stood by the door in the lobby of the hotel and watched the firemen put out the fire. Liam wouldn't let her go outside, but he was out there talking to the sheriff. The stench of burning rubber and smoke was so strong it was hurting her throat. She hadn't gotten the smell out from her senses since the last fire she was involved in.

Liam's car was a write-off, just a shell. She was glued to the spot as she stared out at the chaos and tried to peg down in her discombobulated mind what she was seeing. She opened the glass door as Liam walked toward her.

Even in the rain there were onlookers behind the barriers.

"Your car," she said, "it's a wreck."

"Yeah, not much left of it," he said quietly, simply, and he gently pushed her back inside.

But she didn't want to go back in. She wanted to get out of there, away from there, away from Liam.

He put firm hands on her shoulders until her back met the wall and there was nowhere else for her to go.

"Amelia, you're not going anywhere until we have a little chat. There is no way this is a coincidence. Something else is going on here, and I have a feeling you know exactly what it is."

Liam seemed to know what she was thinking, which

was very annoying.

He had to lean down a little so he could look her straight in the eye. She tried to keep her eyes down, but he used his fingers to raise her chin, and she had no choice but to stare back at him.

"But first I'm getting you the hell out of here before something else happens."

It was then she realized that he was trembling and she understood that she wasn't the only one who was shocked.

She hadn't spoken to her UKPPS handler in over twelve months, because there hadn't been a need. For the first two years after the trial, Amelia had moved around the UK, but when she'd crossed the Atlantic to the USA it seemed as though she no longer needed her handler.

Although Amy said she'd like to keep in touch with her, it was left that if Amelia needed her all she had to do was ring the number Amy had given her. It was strange though that if Angus Rossi had been released why hadn't Amy told her?

Dread settled deep inside her. The thought of Angus Rossi coming after her was terrifying. Tony had warned her that he would choose his brother over her; he gave her one chance to make herself invisible, and she thought that was what she had done.

Amelia hated that she had dragged Liam into this mess. He didn't even know what was going on. She didn't for sure, but she had a pretty damn good idea that it was her past rearing its ugly head.

Her hands were shaking, and she clasped them together in front of her. But she couldn't hide her fear from him; he seemed to be able to read her like a book.

"Come on," he said.

He took hold of her hand and led her away from the people milling about to the room where she had stayed the night with him.

"Pack your stuff." His voice was calm and his gaze steady as he watched her.

"Liam, I can't go with you. Please, just for once stop being that nice man and let me walk away from you." She spoke with as reasonable a voice as she could manage.

"I want to know why, but at this moment I think we need to pack up and go. Now you have two choices." His voice was firm. "You either come with me willingly, or I'll carry you out of here kicking and screaming."

"You wouldn't dare," she exclaimed with the cynicism of a woman who still thought she was in charge.

"Would you care to try me?" he asked with a certain amount of mockery, but she could see he meant every word.

Disconcerted, she folded her arms and looked at him. "Why are you being like this? Just go away and leave me alone to sort out my problems."

"Ah, so now you're admitting it's your problem?" His eyes narrowed, and the corner of his mouth twisted into an I-knew-I-was-right smirk.

Damn! Now she was the victim of her own lies. She wanted to stamp her foot and shout at him to leave her alone. Amelia was experiencing a gamut of emotions. Her mind tried to compartmentalize them, but it wasn't happening, and she was confusing the hell out of herself as to what to do next.

Liam leaned against the doorframe and crossed his legs at the ankles with his hands shoved into his pockets, looking like a man who shouldn't be dealing with stuff like this. He hadn't shaved, and there was a definite scruff on his face, slightly darker than his tawny brown hair.

He was the epitome of sexiness, and what was even more attractive was that he wasn't one of those men who knew it. For years she had stayed away from any kind of lure to the opposite sex. It had been the most sensible thing to do considering her life and that she might have to disappear at a moment's notice.

Her feelings for Liam confused her, and she tried to fight through the cobwebs of how it felt to be magnetized by this man. Her emotions were so conflicted that she was dizzy with it all.

The frustration of trying so hard not to be attracted to Liam assailed her dizzied senses. She was at a point now where she didn't know what was real and what wasn't, and she couldn't control the spasmodic trembling within her.

"I can protect you, Amelia." His voice was gentle as he walked over to where she stood. "I won't let anything happen to you."

And without rhyme or reason, she fell into his arms. He encircled her body close to his and held her tightly as she sobbed her heart out. Years of fear, tension, and loneliness besieged her shaking body.

And all the while Liam just stood and held her. Not talking. Taking the burden and doing what no one had done in a very long time—standing beside her and allowing her to set free all the terrifying moments past and all those to come in the future, because she knew that one way or another it was going to end.

****

Liam couldn't ever remember a feeling where he wanted to absorb someone else's sadness and pain. It was almost unbearable for him to see Amelia so miserable, so brokenhearted. Whatever had happened in her life was serious.

Fuck. It was slightly unnerving to know that someone was targeting her and he had no idea why. There seemed to be no other explanation for the two attacks that had happened in the last twelve hours. They both had one thing in common…Amelia.

Whoever had destroyed his car was clearly hoping that she would be in it and didn't care who else they hurt in the process. Fortunately, the parking lot had been almost empty because of the weather. On a normal day it would have most certainly killed someone, or more than one person. He had oddly primitive thoughts; the type that wanted to be the protector, to hide her and never let anyone upset her again.

He didn't let go of her until the tears had subsided. Holding onto her shoulders, he looked down at her. As a single tear made its way down her cheek, he lifted his hand and caught it with his thumb before it fell from her chin. He cupped her face, and he saw a woman who for one moment looked so defeated.

"Okay?" he asked gently.

She nodded. "I'm sorry."

Amelia stepped back from him so there was some distance between them. He could see her hands were shaking. When she caught him looking at them she clasped them together. And he saw the defiance crawl back into her by the straightening of her back and the set of her shoulders.

"Look, Liam, I can't bring any more danger to your

door. Perhaps it—"

"Don't even think about finishing that sentence." He didn't want to hear her say it.

"But you have no idea what you're getting into."

It seemed she was more afraid for his safety than her own, but he was having none of it. What kind of person would walk away from her now? He was slightly irritated that she would think that of him. Liam was not that kind of person.

He'd survived many years of having the chance to walk away from the hard cases he took on, the ones where the victims became the pursued, and it had only made him want to fight for them even more. Liam would never turn his back on anyone who was in trouble. That's just the way he was.

Which was why he took pro-bono cases regularly. He made his money from those clients who could afford it, so that he could work with cases that didn't have any financial system in place. And any attorney who worked for him did the same or he didn't want them in his office.

"No, I don't, but once I have you stashed away in a safe place, where you'll be protected, you're going to tell me all there is to know. We can come up with a plan and figure out what will work to stop whatever is going on."

"Liam…"

For a moment, it seemed like she was going to argue with him. But he just looked at her with a stare he hoped would tell her that he wasn't going to take *no* for an answer.

"Thank you," she murmured, and he sighed with relief, because it would make things far easier if she was willing to go with him.

"Go pack your bag."

There was a hard knock at the door, and they both turned simultaneously at the sound. He took a couple of steps, and there was another knock. "It's the sheriff, Seth Tayside," a voice on the other side of the door said.

Liam turned and looked at Amelia. "Okay?" he asked her.

She nodded in agreement.

Liam had known that the sheriff would want to question Amelia again. The man had said as much when Liam had spoken to him earlier. And after all, what kind of a law enforcement officer would he be if he wasn't thorough?

As he opened the door he could feel the pensive vibes coming from Amelia. He knew she was thinking of ways to disappear, and he would be watching her like a hawk.

"Sheriff." He opened the door wider for him to enter.

"Mr. Miller," he said as he stepped inside the room.

They shook hands, and Liam could sense that the sheriff wasn't at all happy about the situation. And quite rightly so.

Liam couldn't figure out if Amelia was going to tell the sheriff anything of what had happened, or if she even knew. He looked at her face, and he suspected that if she was involved, she wasn't going to divulge anything at this point.

****

"Miss Bailey." The sheriff nodded to her as he removed his hat and held it in his hands. They were large, just like everything else about this man. She estimated his age to be around hers, perhaps a couple of years older.

Amelia got the sense that he was a hard man, but

fair. He'd come into the café for coffee and muffins, and although they'd spoken in passing they'd never really had a conversation.

She glanced out the window and saw that the car lot was still blocked off. The firemen were rolling up their hoses as the fire was out and the smoke was dissipating.

There were a few spectators who were staring at the scene with inquisitiveness and probably dismay because nothing like this had ever happened in Cape Charles.

"Miss Bailey, it seems that we need to have another talk. You're certainly keeping me busy." He didn't smile but did, however, have a modicum of sincerity in his eyes.

"I'm sorry, Sheriff. I'm not sure what I can tell you." Looking at him, she knew he could tell that she was lying, and she hated that.

"Any boyfriends in the picture?"

"No," she answered.

"What about old ones, or someone that you've upset?"

She shook her head. "Not that I'm aware of." Amelia bit the inside of her cheek. She became increasingly uneasy under his scrutiny. And without thinking, she looked at Liam only to find that he was watching her, his eyes narrowed as if he knew she was lying.

"Sheriff, I think that Amelia is in shock, and if she knew anything about what was going on, she wouldn't be able to tell you."

"Uh-huh, perhaps," he said while watching her intently. He turned to Liam. "Do you think it's anything to do with you, an old case?"

Liam shook his head. "I don't think so. But I guess

anything is possible."

The sheriff frowned. "Umm, seems very odd to me that Miss Bailey would be involved in both incidents unless it was something to do with her."

He was looking at both of them as if expecting an answer, but neither of them spoke. She didn't know what to say, and the silence seemed to last forever, but it was only a few seconds before the sheriff spoke again.

"CSU is on the scene now. I doubt they'll find anything, but who knows?" He shrugged his shoulders. "There may be a print if we're lucky, or something that might tell us what was used. What are your plans at the moment?" he asked her.

"I was thinking of taking Amelia to a cabin up at Beech Mountain," Liam said without looking at her.

That was the first she'd heard of it! However, she could see that it would be a way of getting away from what was going on. Then she could leave when Liam wasn't around.

"I'd rather you didn't take her anywhere until this investigation is over. Now, we need to question Miss Bailey. There seems to be a discrepancy on her visa." He looked at her as he spoke. She could see that he wouldn't let this drop, and what did she expect? After all, he was the law.

"Forget it, not going to happen. Whatever is going on, she's not safe here."

Shit! There was only one thing she could do that would allow her to go.

"Have you got a pen and a piece of paper?" she asked the sheriff.

He frowned then removed a pen and a notebook from his top pocket and handed them to her. And without looking at Liam, although she could feel the air of confusion that was coming from him, she flipped open the pad and clicked the pen on, writing the name of her handler and a series of numbers.

Amelia hesitated a little before she handed it back. This was the first time she'd shown any inclination of what she had gone through.

"Ring this number, it will explain everything."

He glanced down at the pad and nodded. "I'll step outside for a moment." He'd already pulled out his cell before opening the door to leave the room.

She could see the confusion on Liam's face. Disconcerted, she crossed her arms and pointedly looked away. Everything was getting out of hand, and she was almost certain it was all because of her.

"So, am I going to be the last person who finds out what the hell is going on here?" His voice was quiet yet held authority and low tones of anger.

They exchanged a long, deep look. How did this get so complicated so quickly? For so long she'd been in charge, even before she'd succeeded to get herself into all this trouble. Amelia had prided herself on being a strong, independent woman. Now she didn't know who she was, but most of all she didn't want to be the one who held back because of her own stupidity while other people suffered because of her.

"I'm sorry, Liam. I've dragged you into something that is not your concern. And as soon as the sheriff comes back, I'll be gone."

He didn't get a chance to reply because her phone started to buzz, and she knew who it would be. Confirmation of that was on the screen.

The sheriff entered the room as she sent a text to

Amy, telling her that she would ring her as soon as she could, then turned the phone off.

Amy Black was her handler. They hadn't spoken in a year, but despite that, if Angus was out of prison, why hadn't she let Amy know that Angus was out of prison?

"You're in a tough situation, Miss Bailey. If there's anything we can do here, let us know." And with that, he handed her a card with his number on it. "Anytime day or night."

"Thank you," she said, slipping his business card into the back pocket of her jeans.

"I'm not happy about you leaving, but I understand," he said with quiet emphasis. "Mr. Miller, perhaps you could give me the address of where you're taking Miss Bailey?"

Amelia waited for him to say he wasn't about to take her anywhere when he spieled off an address. He spoke with a staid calmness, no sign of the anger she thought she'd heard in his tone before.

"Would you like an escort?"

Liam shook his head. "No, thanks. I have some private security meeting us at the cabin."

The sheriff nodded. "Good choice. Often people who are violent like to stick around and see if the damage they've caused is having the desired effect. They get a thrill from seeing everyone clamber about in the devastation that they've inflicted."

This was the first Amelia had heard about private security. As she was trying to figure out how to get away from Liam the sheriff's radio went off and he was needed somewhere else.

The sheriff put his hat on. "Good luck." He slightly dipped his head at her before shaking Liam's hand. "Be careful."

"Thank you, Sheriff," Liam said as he opened the door for him to leave.

As he left, Amelia turned and stood at the window, looking outside.

As soon as he'd gone, Liam came and stood next to her. His arm was touching hers he was so close. She'd heard the anger in his voice before, and quite rightly so, but now she could sense he'd calmed down.

"How about we pack and get out of here as soon as possible?"

She was momentarily speechless as she looked up. "You still want to?"

"Of course. Why would you think otherwise?"

The blue of his eyes was so intense, shining like a piece of cut sapphire, the arch of his eyebrows slightly raised as he watched her.

Amelia was trying to control the quiver in her jaw. How could he still want to help her? He should have been running for the hills.

Turning her around so that they were facing each other, Liam smoothed his hands up and down her arms, and as if reading her mind, he said, "Did you think I would just leave you? What kind of a man do you take me for?"

"God, Liam, you have no idea what's going on. This is no story, this is my life, and it's not going to be good from now on."

"You're right, I do not know at all about the drama that has happened in the last eighteen hours, but on the drive up to the cabin, you're going to be doing a lot of talking."

****

For fuck's sake, what the hell happened!

It had all gone wrong. Fucking internet. The directions had been followed to the letter. The bomb should not have gone off. It was way too early. The bitch should have been inside the car. The detonator must have been faulty.

But there had been something quite mesmerizing about watching the flames spill from the car like the cascading of molten lava. Blending in with everyone else was easy, and there was the unexpected thrill of knowing that no one realized that the person responsible was standing right in front of them.

Holy fuck, it was exhilarating!

Tracking Amelia wherever she went was easy with the GPS tracker, so if she was on the move—which was expected—it would be simple to follow her. She couldn't hide. Soon enough she would discover what suffering was, and oh what fun it would be to watch.

****

Amelia sat back and listened to the wind whistle through the open window. She watched the landscape passing her by as Liam drove the truck that his friend had lent them toward the cabin.

"It was very good of Jarrod to lend you his truck, and for him to bring Misty." She glanced at the back seat to see her cat in a carrier curled up fast asleep. "How long have you been friends?"

Liam had both hands on the steering wheel, with the relaxed pose of a man used to dealing with hectic highways. She could drive but chose not to.

"Since we were around fifteen."

"And Max, he owns the cabin we're going to?"

"Correct. The three of us have been friends since we

were all living in a children's home."

"I'm sorry, I know what that's like."

He looked at her, and she could see the surprise in his eyes.

"Something we both have in common," she said reflectively as she remembered those years with little more than a split second of happiness, and that was the day she was old enough to leave.

"What happened to your parents?" he asked.

"Parent," she murmured. "My mum had breast cancer," she said, her voice fading into a lowered whisper.

"No family, your dad?" he asked as he overtook a large truck and trailer.

The four lanes made her dizzy just sitting there. The thought of having to drive would have terrified her, and she laughed inwardly at how ironic that was.

Her thoughts returned to Liam's question about her father. When she was growing up, she sometimes felt sorry for herself because she didn't have a father. But later in her life she realized she wasn't the only person without one. She had no bitterness anymore about not having a father to take care of her.

"No one, but that was what I was used to once Mum passed away. She was such a brave woman, so independent and kind, caring. I have many happy memories with her that are still vivid in my mind." Amelia did not doubt all that it was her mother's strength that had gotten her through the last eight years.

"How long have you lived in the US?"

"Six years in all, Cape Charles four."

He nodded. She could see that he was mulling that over, so she took the chance to ask him a question.

"What about you, why were you in a home?"

"I lived with an aunt who liked looking at the bottom of a bottle. Then one day she decided she couldn't cope with a teenage boy."

"I'm sorry."

"Don't be, it was the biggest favor anyone had ever done for me, especially her."

His voice held no bitterness as she would have expected it to.

"How far is this cabin?" she asked, trying to hide a yawn. The last few tumultuous days were catching up with her.

"A little over seven hours."

She masked her inner turmoil with a calmness that surprised her.

"So, talk, Amelia. What the hell is going on?"

She searched anxiously for a point where she could begin. Looking over at him, she saw him staring straight ahead, his gaze fixed on the road. It seemed as though he was concentrating on driving, but she knew he would be listening to her.

"I don't even know where to start." A wave of apprehension swept through her. She was nervous as to how he would react. There was no doubt that they had a connection in more ways than one, and he'd been clear from the start that he liked her.

"How about the beginning?" He glanced at her and smiled before looking back at the road.

"I was a very naïve twenty-year-old, extremely shy, and not at all like most women of that age. I had no confidence in me, no belief in my abilities…actually, I didn't think I could do anything worthwhile."

That was the direct result of the part of her life that

had sent her spiraling from the girl who always made top grades in school to the girl who lost the one thing she loved more than anything…her mum. It had always been just the two of them, and when she'd been put in that home, her life changed for the worse, and it seemed she would never recover from it.

Liam didn't speak. He seemed to sense that she wanted to take it slowly, which she appreciated.

"I left school with nothing. All I wanted was to be left alone. I worked in a multitude of different places from clothes stores to petrol stations. That was where I met Tony Rossi."

Amelia stared straight ahead. The traffic was heavy but steady. Liam drove with confidence, and she sensed his experience. He drove with both hands on the wheel, but his elbow was leaning on the edge of his side window.

Taking a deep breath, she leaned her head back onto the seat rest and closed her eyes. Amelia realized that this was the first time she had told her full story, and bloody hell it felt good. She released her breath audibly, and it somehow felt as though she was letting go of all the anxiety that had built up inside her.

"He seemed to take a liking to me, but I kept refusing when he asked me to go out with him."

She still remembered the part of her that was bowled over by his style and good looks.

"One day after I had locked up the shop I went to my usual bus stop to get my ride back to a small studio apartment I was renting at the time. I had turned twenty-one a few weeks earlier." A birthday she had spent on her own. "That day it was pouring down rain, and I'd forgotten my umbrella. A car went through a large puddle, and the water splashed on me. I looked like a drowned rat. The next thing I knew, the driver had stopped and got out apologizing profusely. It was the same man who had asked me out several times when he'd been to put fuel in his car. He insisted on taking me home, and I was..." She pursed her lips. "...overwhelmed by this guy. He was tall and so good-looking." She shook her head. "And that was the start of Tony Rossi and everything that happened thereafter."

For the first time since she'd started telling her story, Liam spoke. "How about a break? Would you like a coffee?"

"Yes," she said with a certain amount of relief.

They'd just entered the state of North Carolina when Liam took an exit off the highway. He seemed to know where he was going, because within five minutes they'd pulled into the parking lot of what looked like a rest stop.

Reaching down for her purse, Amelia opened her door and climbed out of the truck. Liam came around the hood to stand beside her.

"Do you want to sit inside, or at one of the picnic tables?"

"Outside," she said. "I'll take Misty in her carrier so she can get some fresh air, and see if she wants some water and food."

Liam opened the back passenger side door and reached in for the carrier. He also took a brown paper bag out and handed it to her.

"Mrs. Jameson put a few things in there she thought you might need for Misty."

Amelia was overwhelmed by her neighbor's kindness. She took it and had to hold back the tear that was precariously threatening to spill over.

Liam rubbed her arm. "Come on, honey."

They walked toward the nearest seat, and she put the bag down on the table. He set the carrier down beside her.

"Coffee?"

She nodded. "Yes please." Amelia opened her purse, but before she could get her wallet out, Liam laid his hand over hers to stop her.

"I'll get them."

"Thanks."

"How about something to eat? You've hardly eaten at all."

"I'm not hungry," she said.

He inclined his head and met her gaze. "Really?" He drew his eyebrows together.

"Really," she said.

"Well, I'm starving, so how about a bagel each?" he asked, not listening to her.

"Fine," she agreed, knowing that it would be futile to argue with him.

Liam walked to the building, and Amelia opened the bag and took out the dish and a bottle of water. Crouching down, she unhooked the door of the carrier and put her hand in to stroke the cat's fur.

"Hey, kitty, are you all right?"

Meow, meow. Misty pushed her head against the palm of Amelia's hand, and she complied by scratching the cat's neck. Pouring the water into the dish, she set it in front of the cat and she lapped up some.

Looking inside the bag, she saw some of Misty's favorite treats. Taking some out, she set them on the floor of the carrier. Luckily, Misty was small and had plenty of room. She ate one of the treats, but Amelia could tell that her little kitty was not happy. And who could blame her?

This was why she should never have had anything that needed her. She knew in the back of her mind that this day would come. Taking the dish out and throwing the water away, Amelia closed the door of the carrier. Misty stared back at her, looking miserable. Amelia lifted the carrier and set it on the bench beside her and waited for Liam to return.

The sun was warm on her face, but there was a breeze. She took a band from her wrist and tied her hair up. Once they were back on the road she would ring Amy. She did have a handler when she was handed to the WISTEC team, but Amelia preferred Amy; she trusted her.

Perhaps she was just being overly cautious, but she somehow thought not. She had the beginnings of a headache, and she pressed her fingers to her forehead and rubbed the skin.

"Bloody hell," she whispered.

Chapter 7

Liam walked toward Amelia with two coffees and a couple of breakfast bagels. She needed to eat. He could see the strain on her face as he got to the table where she was sitting. She was nervously tapping her fingers on the tabletop when she glanced in his direction. Smiling, she clasped her hands in front of her as if trying to hide her feelings.

He set a coffee and bag in front of her. "Eat," he said. "And then perhaps you might feel up to telling me the rest of your story."

He sat down opposite her. Their knees touched, and he knew she had felt that zing of chemistry, because she looked at him, and her eyes—her beautiful green eyes—held surprise in them.

He watched her as she took the lid off her coffee and sipped it, then she unwrapped her bagel and ate it without saying a word. He didn't speak either, sensing that she needed the quiet time. When they had both finished he took the trash to the litter bin, then sat back down opposite her to finish his coffee.

"How's Misty?" he asked.

"Miserable." She half-laughed.

"Poor thing. Hopefully, she'll sleep the rest of the way. I'm hoping not to stop again except for bathroom breaks."

"That's fine with me." She smiled briefly.

"Are you ready to talk a bit more about what's going on?" Liam noticed how tired she seemed, and he hated to see the hurt on her face, but for him to help her, he needed to understand what the hell was going on.

Amelia smiled at him as if understanding and nodded. She averted her gaze for a second. There was a myriad of sadness, fear, and regret in her expression. To have all those emotions at once must be so overwhelming. It frightened him as to what she was going to say.

"It's so hard for me to speak about this part of my life…you have no idea."

"No, I don't, but I want to help."

"The guy that stopped that day?"

He nodded, reaffirming that he remembered.

"His name was Tony Rossi, and we fell in love, or I thought we did. He and I had different ideas about what love meant, I realize that now."

She glanced his way. Her voice was laden with emotion, and as much as he didn't want to put her through what seemed to be a roller coaster ride of emotions, he had to know the truth.

"Tony belonged to one of the most notorious families in London who were the center of the London gangs. I didn't know that until it was too late." Her voice was suddenly bitter, and she buried her nose in her cup as she sipped her coffee as if she was trying to avoid looking at him.

He'd heard of the Rossi family, and read about them in the newspaper. They were notorious even here.

"Were you both serious?" he asked.

"We were engaged."

"That is serious," he said, trying to hold back the

possessive desire he suddenly felt.

"His family was…let's just say they were hard to get on with. They didn't like me. His mother thought I wasn't good enough for one of her boys."

"Boys?"

"Yeah, he had an older brother, Angus." Drinking the last of her coffee, she put the lid back on. "Are you finished with yours?"

Liam nodded, and she picked it up and strolled over to the trash can. It was as if she needed a moment to get herself together. He tilted his head to one side as he watched the sway of her hips. It didn't matter what she wore, but he did like her in jeans. She had a very womanly figure, and he enjoyed that she had curves. Her waist was small and her ass rounded.

Liam looked away and rubbed his hand across his cheek, feeling the growth of his unshaven face. He hated to see her in so much pain as she spoke. There was a resilience about her that made him think she had been made to grow up very quickly.

Returning to the table, she sat back down. "The night that Tony and I were going to tell his family about our engagement, he was supposed to pick me up from work. But Tony got caught up and asked Angus to pick me up. I wasn't happy, but what could spoil how I felt? I was in love."

Liam was considering all that she was telling him, and quite frankly, he was scared at how it was going to end, because evidently, it did not have a happy conclusion.

"After Angus picked me up he said he had to stop and see someone that was on the way." She swallowed and closed her eyes for a moment before opening them and looking at him.

A muscle quivered in her jaw, and his gut clenched.

"He was gone such a long time that I went looking for him. God, I wished I'd stayed in the car. Angus was arguing with someone, and as I got closer I could hear that it was becoming violent. But still, I carried on instead of going back."

Amelia shook her head as if she still couldn't believe she hadn't turned tail and gone back to the car.

"I was just in time to witness Angus pulling a knife out and stabbing the man."

"And he saw you?"

She nodded. "Yes, but I turned and ran as fast as I could. Fortunately, there were two policemen on walking duty."

Liam put both his hands around hers that were laying on top of the table. He saw the look of surprise on her face, but he felt he needed to show Amelia that he was there.

"Let me guess, you had to be a witness for the prosecution?"

She nodded. "I was under UKPPS protection. Angus received a life sentence for murder, but he's eligible for parole in twenty-five years. Tony hated me. It was like he had become this totally different person. I stayed in the UK for about a year after the trial, moving from place to place, but I was terrified."

A tremor touched her lips, and he was barely able to stop himself from gathering her up in his arms.

"My handler, Amy, suggested that I should consider leaving the country. Which was what I did, and that was six years ago. I moved around a little but finally settled in Cape Charles."

"Are you in the WISTEC program here?"

"No, Amy wanted me to, but I preferred just to completely reinvent myself."

"Is Amelia your real name?"

"Yes, it's just my last name that is different. I'm Bailey here, but my real surname is Rose."

"So, what are you saying? Angus is out of prison?"

"Or perhaps Tony is seeking revenge and has managed to find me," she murmured. "It's highly unlikely that Angus is out of prison after only ten years."

"Let me see what I can find out." He knew a few people. As a criminal law attorney he'd worked with the WISTEC program before.

Liam had no idea what he'd been expecting her to say, but that sure as hell wasn't what he'd expected.

Holy fuck!

"I need to ring Amy back once we are on the move."

"Okay, let's get on our way."

He came around the table and picked up the carrier. Liam stood with his hand outstretched to help her up. She took his hand, and he squeezed hers. When she stood, instead of releasing her hand, he kept hold of it. For a moment he felt her hesitation, and then he smiled as her fingers curled around his. It felt good as they walked back to the truck. She fitted him like a glove.

"Everything is going to be fine." He offered her a smile, and although hesitant, she returned it.

****

Once they were back on the road and they had traveled for about ten minutes, Amelia checked to make sure Misty was settled, then took out her phone. She scrolled through her contacts until she came to Amy's number and pressed *dial*.

Looking at her watch, she saw that it was ten after two in the afternoon. She mentally counted back five hours to the time in London. It would be just after nine a.m., and she was confident that her handler would already be at her desk.

As she held the phone to her ear and waited while the ringing tone sounded, she stretched her legs out in front of her. This was the day she had dreaded coming.

The call was answered on the second ring. "Amelia, are you all right?" There was concern in her voice.

"Hi, Amy. Yes, I'm fine."

"I don't think that's the truth." Amy's English accent sounded strange to Amelia's ears after all this time, even though she'd spoken briefly to her earlier on.

"What's going on, Amy? I thought Angus had at least another fifteen years to go?"

"He does, and he's still in prison."

"Really?"

"Yes, and Tony is here in London running the family business. We had eyes on him this morning."

The family—which consisted of Tony, Angus, and their mother—had several jewelry stores around the UK. They were high-end, and only the rich could afford to shop there.

"Someone is definitely after me, two incidents, same MO, or am I being insanely jumpy?"

"No, you're not, but we don't know who it is. You've hidden fairly well, but it seems as though you may have been discovered, but by whom we have no idea."

"Great," Amelia said with disdain sharpening her tone.

"We're doing our best and are working with the

United States Marshals to try to figure out what's happening."

"I'm sorry for being sharp. I just can't believe that after all this time I'm on the run again."

She heard Amy draw in a deep breath. "I know, but we're doing everything we possibly can. I'm sending some officers to pick you up."

"No point, Amy. I'm on the move."

"Where?"

"Actually, somewhere on Beech Mountain, but I don't have the address yet. Hold on, I'll pass you to Liam, and yes, before you ask, I trust him."

Liam looked at her and smiled. He'd stayed quiet throughout her conversation. She handed him the phone and he spoke to Amy.

"Hi, Amy. I'm Liam Miller."

She heard him say that he was a criminal law attorney in Washington, DC, and she guessed Amy was asking him what he did and where he lived. Amelia knew that Amy would be doing a background check on him as they spoke.

They spoke for a few moments more before he gave the address where they would be staying. He listened to what was being said on the other end before passing the phone back to her.

"Amy?"

"Amelia, you take care." There was a slight pause. "Don't trust anyone until we have this figured out."

"I won't. Speak soon."

Amelia pressed the *end call* button and put the phone back in her purse.

She sat for a moment, undecided on what to say or do next. Turning her head, she looked at the man who was literally her modern-day hero, and yet he had no idea. It was as if it would be ridiculous to think he'd act any other way. He drove with ease, but there was a tenseness evident that wasn't normally there, and she guessed that was her fault.

"I'm sorry," she said, feeling nervous and sad at the same time. How had she managed to drag him into all of this? But he shocked her by reaching over and snagging her hand with his, squeezing it before letting it go.

"You have nothing to be sorry about. This was my choice."

"You didn't really have one," she said with sadness. This was what she had wanted to avoid. It was her problem, no one else's, and guilt rippled down her spine. "You can still drop me off somewhere. You know this isn't the first time I've been in this position."

"Not a chance." He glanced at her briefly and smiled before returning his gaze to the road. As he switched on the turn signal, indicating to overtake a large truck, he said with a determined tone, "You are stuck with me whether you like it or not."

Amelia wondered what he was like in the courtroom. One thing was for sure, she felt safe with him, and the astonishment was that she had never had the pleasure or the luxury of that with anyone. And she did like it—she liked it a lot.

"Why don't you try to nap for a bit? We have a few hours left of driving."

She did feel tired. She hadn't had a full night's sleep in a while.

"You don't mind?"

"Of course not. I wouldn't have suggested it otherwise."

As he spoke she felt a strange lurch of her heart. This man was getting under her skin, and in a good way. Amelia knew it from the moment she'd laid eyes on him, but ignoring it had been nigh-on impossible.

Could she really trust her judgment after what had happened the last time she'd had feelings for someone? Amelia had no idea what was going to happen in her life, and the thought of anyone else suffering because of her was completely horrifying to her.

"Why don't you put the seat back and relax?" Liam murmured.

"Okay, thanks." She reached beneath her and pulled the handle, which set her half-back. Laying her head against the leather, she felt her eyes getting sleepy. They were gritty and sore, and she hadn't realized just how tired she was.

Amelia was beginning to understand how deeply she had kept her secret. Living in Cape Charles she had buried her wounds and had always hoped that they would stay that way.

Ironically, the stability that she had searched for her whole life, she had found, and now she feared that she would lose everything she had fought to treasure. Which left her wondering if she was going to survive whatever the future held for her.

She didn't know if running was going to be an option. It seemed that the choice had been taken away from her by whoever it was that had discovered her whereabouts. Only time would tell, the time it seemed she didn't have a lot of. Amelia just hoped to God that no one else got hurt in the process of her fighting to stay alive.

****

Liam drove up the long drive to Max's cabin. His friend had been on vacation here with his new wife and her nephew. Liam had spoken to Max while Amelia had been sleeping. His friend said he'd wait until they got there before he left.

Liam saw Max's SUV parked outside the cabin, and he pulled up beside it. At one time the cabin had been just one room, but Jarrod and himself had helped Max expand it, making it into a stunning place to come any time of the year.

"Amelia." Liam put his hand on her shoulder and gently shook it.

She opened her eyes.

"We're here," he said as she straightened up and rolled her shoulders.

"Sorry, I didn't mean to sleep for that long."

"You needed it," he said as he unbuckled his seatbelt. She did the same, and he saw her looking around.

"This looks very nice." She sounded surprised, and he smiled.

"What did you expect?"

"I don't know. When you said *cabin* I envisaged just a wooden shed type thing."

Liam chuckled. "It was like that once upon a time."

He opened the door and got out. Stretching his arms above his head, he was glad to unfold himself from the sitting position.

Opening the side door, he took Misty out. "We'll come back out for our bags in a moment. Come and meet Max and his family."

Amelia joined him, although he noted she stood quite a bit behind him. The door opened before he got there and out came his friend.

"Max, how are you, bud?" Liam said, smiling.

"I'm good," he said as they shook hands and Liam patted Max on the back.

"Max, this is Amelia, the girl I was telling you about."

She held out a hand and his friend took it, shaking it warmly.

"Thank you for allowing me to stay here." She tilted her head and smiled.

"A friend of Liam's is always welcome here. Come and meet my wife."

She tentatively cleared her throat. "Thank you."

Liam put a hand on the small of her back, and she gave him a tense smile. They walked up the two steps to the surrounding porch and stepped inside the open double doors.

"Uncle Liam!"

He laughed as the little boy flew into his open arms. It was a good thing he'd set Misty's carrier on the floor.

"Hey, Charlie. How you doin', buddy?"

"We have been staying here on holiday," he said to Liam, his English accent prominent. Max had met his wife in Chester, England.

"Jeez, when are you going to stop growing?" Liam said as he put Charlie down.

"I'm six now," he said with a proud look on his face.

"You're positively old," Liam said, laughing.

"Ooo, a cat. We have one at home." Charlie flopped onto his stomach on the floor and poked his fingers in the carrier.

"Liam, how are you?"

"Talia," he said as she came toward him with her

arms open. "I'm good. How are you?" he asked, wrapping her up in a hug.

"I'm fantastic, thank you."

"Talia, this is my friend Amelia."

"Lovely to meet you," she said.

Liam smiled when Talia hugged her. He was glad that Max's wife had greeted her so warmly, because he could feel the uneasiness coming from Amelia in vibes.

"Is she your girlfriend?" Charlie asked him.

"Not yet," he answered.

"What does that mean?" he asked, a frown appearing between his baby brown eyes.

"It means that he's tried and she has refused him," Max said, laughing, and ruffled the little boy's hair.

Liam playfully punched Max on the arm. "Hey, you're making me sound like a loser."

"That's because you are," Max said, grinning.

Charlie turned to Amelia and spoke to her, "I can't say your name. I've been trying in my head, but it's all wrong."

Amelia looked at the little boy with a smile on her face. "It's okay, Charlie, you can call me Milly."

"Milly…yes," he said as he got up from the floor and started skipping around. "I can say that."

Liam chuckled, and Max told Charlie to settle down.

"Let me show you where everything is," Talia said to Amelia.

Amelia looked at Liam. He couldn't quite read the expression in her eyes, but he nodded so that she would know she was safe. A small smile found its way through a mask of uncertainty. He hated that she was feeling that way.

"Give me a hand with our suitcases," Max said to

Liam. "I swear Talia packs enough for months instead of weeks."

Liam could see the love in the eyes of his friend for the woman he'd fallen for and quite clearly adored. It made him so very happy for Jarrod and Max that they had both found their forever happiness.

"Sure," Liam said as he picked up two cases.

After they had packed up Max's SUV, the two of them stood and leaned against the vehicle while chatting.

"Are you going to be all right?" Max asked after Liam had told him more about what was going on.

"Yeah, the US Marshals are taking the lead on this. Amelia trusts her handler, Amy, but she lives in the UK." Liam folded his arms as he thought for a moment of the danger he might be stepping into. But he had no doubt in his mind that he wanted to protect Amelia. "The National Crime Officers in the UK may have some input as to what has happened," Liam said, frowning.

"You understand something of what is going on, you've dealt with WISTEC before with some of your clients. Do you think she should go into the program?"

"I don't know, Max. I haven't even had a chance to discuss it with her yet."

Just then Amelia, Talia, and Charlie came out of the house.

"Come on, bud, get in," Max said to Charlie. "Take care, Liam, and if you need anything, you know where I am."

Liam stood and watched them go before turning around to walk toward Amelia. They needed to have that talk. He scrubbed his hand over his face; he felt exhausted.

****

Amelia watched as Liam came toward her. His body was lithe, his hair shone in the sun, and he walked with confidence. The large oak tree to her right was gently swaying in the breeze, the leaves still green, but she knew that very soon they would be a vibrant orange as fall descended upon them.

There were pink rhododendrons along the pathway to the cabin and in between those were white hydrangea bushes. She could see flowers that she didn't know the name of but they were beautifully cerise pink with an amazing scent of sweet roses. There was a trace of pine, and she breathed it deep into her lungs.

She stood on the decking, the Juliet balcony that covered the two floors making her feel safe. As Liam came to stand beside her, she watched him close his eyes for a moment as if taking in every scent and sound.

Then he turned to her. "Let's get Misty settled in, and I'll show you where you'll be sleeping."

"Thank you, Liam."

"No problem," he said as he headed back inside the house.

"No." She put her hand on his arm to stop him. "Thank you for helping me. You're very brave. I'm sure—no, I'm *very* sure—you really don't understand what letting me stay here may entail. You still have time to back out. It might be for the best," she concluded.

He stood looking down at her. Amelia couldn't read his expression, and she wondered if he was going to back out like she had just suggested.

"I'd never do that," he said as he drew her into his arms and held her close to him for a moment.

She breathed in his scent. Not particularly a cologne type, but a warm, clean, safe fragrance. She looked up at him, meeting his eyes with her own.

He smiled before running a hand over his hair. "Come on," he said, keeping one arm around her while they both walked back into the house.

As he shut the large, double glass doors, she heard the sound of the key in the lock and the bolt being turned. He was being cautious, which was good. She had no idea what to expect, but if it was anything to go by what had already happened...

She crouched down to Misty's carrier and stroked the cat on the chin. She had been so good.

"Let's take her to the kitchen and put some water and food out for her." Liam picked up the carrier as she stood up and followed him.

Amelia realized that the downstairs floor was pretty much one massive room, set into sections by the furniture. It was so open, and yet for such a large space, it was homely.

There was an enormous, circle dining table in a light pine wood, with ten chairs around it. The focal point of the room, without a doubt, was the open log fireplace. It was like nothing she'd ever seen before. It was huge with logs piled on either side.

The theme of the room was light and airy with plenty of pastel colors. Except for the sofas, and there were three of them, which were covered in a mushroom fabric that looked soft and comfortable with plenty of cushions and throws. She was so exhausted she felt like she could just melt into one. There was an oval rug in the center. Its abstract design had an array of colors defining its shape, which was set on the beautifully polished wooden floor.

"If we just let Misty out, she can get a sense of

what's about her," Liam said as he placed the carrier on the floor and opened the door.

Misty just sat inside, sniffing the air. So Amelia coaxed her out with a treat she'd taken from the bag. It did the trick, and her fur baby stepped out, all be it tentatively to begin with. But the scent of her favorite treat got the better of her, and she took it from Amelia's hand with her mouth. Sniffing the air, she moved slowly as she explored her temporary home.

"I asked Talia to get some things for us, and she picked up some food and a litter tray for Misty."

"You're so kind. Thank you."

"Amelia."

"Yes." She stood up and turned to him, frowning.

"Stop saying thank you…there's no need."

"I'm sorry." She stole a look at him as she chewed her bottom lip.

"Hey," he said as he caught hold of her shoulders. "Why don't you finish setting things up for Misty, I'm going to make you a cup of tea to take to your room with you. I want you to sleep for a bit. I'll wake you up when I have dinner ready."

"That doesn't seem fair," she said, trying to keep her heartbeat under control. Every time Liam came near, her heart rate liked to go at a speed that was not conducive to everyday living.

"What, you don't think I can cook?" he said with a half-smile.

"No, I didn't say that at all." And she realized she'd spoken with an irate tone.

"I'm teasing you," he said as he drew her closer.

"I know. I'm sorry. Lack of sleep," she said.

"And stop saying *sorry*, you don't have to keep

apologizing all the time."

Leaning her head with a thump on his chest, she let out a big sigh. If she was being forward by getting closer to him, it was not her concern now. Liam was right, she needed sleep.

The thought of the two very violent attacks so close together made her throat go dry, and she couldn't summon up enough saliva to swallow down the grittiness. Liam must be feeling the strain as well, but he showed no signs of it. She wasn't a weak person, not by any means. She could fight, and she had and would again to keep her life.

Her courage and determination to fight for herself were like a rock in her stomach. All she needed was some more sleep and she'd be ready for whatever was coming her way. Amelia had no idea who was after her, but one thing she knew one hundred percent was that it had something to do with the Rossi family.

The last ten years had been lived in a state of fear, and she'd had enough of it. One way or another this situation was going to be resolved, and she would do whatever she had to.

Liam kissed the top of her head. They had become so close in the last twenty-four hours, and that seemed so surreal…for her anyway.

"Come on, let's get you settled in."

Chapter 8

Once Liam left the room Amelia shut the door and pressed her forehead against it as she tried to control the emotions running rife through her body. How she'd kept herself from crumbling into a heap on the ground she had no idea.

Liam's friends were so nice, and she didn't deserve them. If they had only realized what could happen, they would have never let her in the door. She could see by Liam's face that he loved those people she'd just met. They were clearly like family to him.

Amelia was worried that what was going on in her life would put everyone Liam knew at risk. Things between them were new, and in a normal situation, they would have time to explore them. However, this wasn't normal, and she should still stick to her plan and leave Liam behind.

She frowned. It surprised her that in such a short time Liam had come to mean a lot to her. She couldn't explain why or how that had happened, but it had.

The fact of the matter was that the person who had it in for her had been watching her, because they knew about Liam, which was evident when they had blown up his car. Amelia shuddered. It could have been so much worse than it had been.

Why was this happening now, when she had finally gotten her life in order? And who was it? Angus was still in prison, and Tony was in London. Although with the type of people the brothers mixed with, it could be anyone.

Sitting down on the side of the bed, she sighed and rubbed the back of her neck. The opulently colored throw beneath her and varied pillows matched the ottoman at the bottom of the bed. The accent of honeysuckles seemed to be the theme in this bedroom. It was light and surprisingly big.

Facing her was another door. Amelia stood, walked over to the ajar door, and pushed it open. She found an en-suite with a large corner shower, that was quite simply humongous, and a free-standing tub. There were twin wash basins with a large mirror above them. The richness of the yellow and white was accented with the matching towels and accessories. Whoever had decorated it had an excellent eye.

Amelia didn't want to rest, but she did need to have a long, hot shower, which was what she did. It was like washing away all her mind's thoughts of the last two days, and she just stood there and let the water run over her.

After she'd dried herself and pulled some jeans and a plain white t-shirt out of her bag, she put her clothes on before opening the sliding glass doors that led out onto the balcony. There was even a porch swing to her left. She leaned on the wooden lattice rail.

The view was impressive. Miles of forestry, mountains, and what looked like a ski slope. The colors of fall were starting to appear faster here than in Cape Charles. The sun was still out, but the air was getting colder, and she shivered, taking one last look before she turned to go inside and get a sweater.

She should have realized that she had gotten way too complacent. When something like this happened in your life it was impossible to let go of the fear.

It was the fear that kept you on your toes. And she had relaxed and let her guard down. It was a stupid thing to do.

She used to be a placid, easy-going girl, but what she had been through had turned her into a woman who didn't give in easily to anybody or anything. She seriously needed to pull herself together and find out who the hell was targeting her.

Amelia hated that she had put other lives in danger, and not just from the fire but the car bombing; a man she seemed to have feelings for…that was a whole other story because she didn't know where those unexpected emotions had come from.

Amelia felt bruised, not physically but mentally, and with a vulnerability she did not like. Liam had been like this massive cocoon shielding her from the pain and hurt. His sense of protection was unyielding, and he seemed to think nothing of putting her first.

"Stop it," she muttered to herself. *Stop going around in circles and getting nowhere.*

Her cell started ringing and she took it out of her purse and answered it, recognizing the number.

"Hi, Amy," she said.

Hey, hunny, how are you?" Her voice sounded concerned, and although it had been a long time since Amelia had seen her, she could see Amy's face frowning, full of concern for her.

Amy would be in her mid-fifties now. Her blonde hair and figure to die for had always made Amelia envious. She doubted that Amy had changed much.

Staying in shape wasn't just her passion, but necessary for her job as well. She'd been a self-defense instructor before she'd become part of the UKPPS team.

Amelia had learned many moves from her, but she wasn't even sure if she remembered how to do them. When she was waiting to appear in court, Amy had been assigned to keep her safe. Eight months was a long time to spend with someone when you weren't allowed any other visitors.

"I've been better," Amelia answered. "Do you know what's going on, Amy?"

"I think I've found out who is targeting you."

Amelia's heart was thumping in her chest. "Who?"

"Is your friend Liam there?"

"No, he's downstairs."

"Go get him and put the phone on speaker."

Amy hadn't even finished speaking and Amelia had pulled open the door and raced down the stairs, almost knocking Liam over as she rushed through the living area looking for him. He was in the kitchen chopping a tomato. When he saw her he put the knife down.

"Hey," he said, grabbing hold of her shoulders.

"It's Amy. She knows who is after me." Amelia put the cell on the countertop and set it on speaker. She was barely able to stop the panic buzzing through her body at an alarming rate. An uneasiness was creeping around her like a deadly ivy, and she was struggling to get her breath out.

"Relax," Liam said as he put his arm around her. "Relax. I told you, I've got you."

She breathed in deeply and got herself under some kind of control, but she couldn't stop her heart from banging inside her chest.

****

Liam could hear the uneasiness creeping into Amelia's voice. The tenseness around her mouth told him she was keeping it together. No one could go through what she had and not be strong and in control.

"Have you got a laptop, Liam?" Amy asked through the phone.

"Yeah, sure," he said, letting go of Amelia and going over to the dining table where he had opened it up to answer some emails. He brought it to the countertop and opened it. "I've got it," he said.

"Give me your email address," Amy said.

He did, and he immediately saw a new email pop up in his box. Clicking on the link, he waited for the feed to open on his screen. It was a picture that looked as if it had been taken outside the hotel where he had been staying.

"So, what are we looking at, Amy?" he asked.

"Enlarge the photograph."

He did as she'd instructed.

"Oh my God," Amelia muttered.

"Exactly," Amy said, resonating the tone in Amelia's voice.

"What?" Liam asked. It was obvious that the two women knew. But he was completely in the dark.

"That," Amelia said, pointing to a slightly blurry image of a woman watching what was going on when the bomb exploded in his car. "That is Angus Rossi's mother."

"Mother? You're kidding me?" he exclaimed.

She shook her head. "Nope, we aren't."

"Dear God. You mean she's the one who set fire to your kitchen and then set a bomb on my car?" He couldn't believe it. The woman in the picture was about sixty with short, gray hair and a slim build.

"It seems very coincidental that she would be at the scene when your car exploded. I'd say she's been searching for Amelia since her testimony sent her son to prison."

"But that was eight years ago," Amelia said, the panic becoming more evident in her voice.

"Okay, so what do we do next?" Liam asked.

"You don't. Amelia is our priority. Just keep her safe until I can get the US Marshals to you."

"She never liked me," Amelia said. "I'm not at all surprised. She adored her sons, but it was very clear that she oversaw them and what they did."

There was a long pause before Amy spoke. "We're gathering as much data as we can. Unfortunately, even after going through CCTV, we can't locate her. It would appear as though she's vanished."

Liam certainly did not like the sound of that.

"How long before the marshals are here?" he asked.

"Within twenty-four hours. Then they will take Amelia into custody."

"Not a chance," he said vehemently.

"Liam." Amelia put her hand on his arm. "It will be best. Ivy Rossi is not a woman to toy with. Don't underestimate what she's capable of."

"No." He couldn't help the possessiveness in his voice. There was no way she was moving from his side. "I can protect her. They can come here, but she stays right by my side." He surprised himself at how determined he was to protect her.

Liam could be stubborn, both inside and outside of the courtroom. It was exactly that kind of determination, clear thinking, and positive attitude that made him good at his job.

Amelia's eyes widened as she looked up at him. "This isn't like being in court, Liam. These people are dangerous. She is dangerous."

"Do you think I don't know that? I was there both times, remember?"

He had a gun, and he knew how to use it. In his line of work, he had a few enemies that he'd put in prison. Max, Jarrod, and himself had gotten involved with boxing. He knew how to fight, and he wouldn't hesitate to use his skills to protect Amelia.

"Do you feel safe with me?" he asked her.

"Yes, of course I do," she said without any hesitation.

"Okay, Amy, it's settled. I'm expecting my team here within the next few hours."

"Affirmative," Amy said. "But please be careful, both of you."

"We will." Liam terminated the call.

Amelia had gone to stand by the French doors, looking out onto the long garden. He came up behind her and turned her around. He lowered his head so that he could see her eyes. Her expression was grim, and he led her to the couch where she sat next to him.

"Ivy Rossi is the person who firebombed us and blew up my car, right?" Liam said.

"I do not doubt that it's her. I don't know why she didn't cross my mind before. I just assumed because it had been so long ago, that I was safe." Her voice sounded fairly calm considering what was going on in her life. "Don't let her age fool you into thinking that she's going to be easy to stop. She is a formidable person, and tough."

"And clearly psychopathic." Liam knew that this was not just a mother protecting her son—this was revenge. He could feel the taut lines of Amelia's body next to him, and he wanted to wrap her up so close to him that it would be impossible for anyone to get near her.

"What are we going to do?" she asked.

"Nothing," he muttered. "This cabin has the best alarm system money can buy. And it has the advantage of having only one way in and out. No one can come here without us knowing."

Liam pulled out his cell and typed a few texts. Almost immediately he received replies.

"What are you planning?" she asked, looking worried.

"I have some contacts in security. King Group Investigative Services. I've met one of the owners several times, Micah King. I want to update him."

"And what is he going to do?"

"Well, to start, he's going to see if he can find this woman. My guess is that she's so intent on hurting you that she's not going to be too careful about where she is and what she's doing. Chances are that she doesn't even think you'd realize it is her," he said, hoping that his voice was calmer than he felt.

"Why not just rely on the marshals?" Amelia asked.

"Because they don't have the money or resources to give you their undivided time."

"But Amy said they would be here within twenty-four hours."

"And what about now? Are they looking for Ivy Rossi at this moment?" he said with quiet emphasis.

139

"Maybe."

Liam didn't think she sounded all that confident.

"We're going to stop this woman. You're safe with me," he said.

****

But at what cost? Amelia didn't want anyone to get hurt because of her past. Liam was one of those people who took care of everyone and everything.

She imagined how the fire in front of her would look when it was lit…so romantic, snuggly and warm. Large logs of wood spitting. And a glow of warmth would have settled over them. She could feel the tautness of his muscles as his thigh leaned against hers.

When she looked up at him she noticed he was watching her intently. His jaw was almost covered in growth, but it didn't hide that sexy dimple on his chin. She was fighting a need to just wrap herself inside his strong arms and lay her head on his chest.

It made her very conscious of how virile and sexy he was; it wasn't an emotion she should be having right now, but she couldn't help it. At this moment Amelia just wanted to forget about her life and what was happening.

Misty was asleep on the window ledge, curled up into a ball. She had settled in amazingly well.

Liam's phone dinged and he took it from his pocket. After looking at the message, he frowned.

"Where's your phone?"

"Over on the counter."

He got up and she twisted around to see what he was doing.

"What's wrong?" she asked as he picked it up.

"Micah just texted me to check it."

"For what?" she asked.

"A tracker." He took the back off, slid the sim card out, and took out something else, which was tiny.

"What's that?" she asked with a slight alarm in her voice.

"Holy shit," he muttered.

"What?" She almost screamed the word at him.

"It's a tracker."

Amelia felt all the blood drain from her face. "How did that get inside my phone?"

"I'm guessing that someone got close enough to you to take your phone, and they put it back before you noticed."

"Oh my God. Where, how?"

"The café?" he asked as he put it on the kitchen countertop.

Dear God, she left her phone in the back where they hung their coats, and she guessed someone could very easily come in a back way and retrieve it.

Liam came back over to sit by her and picked his cell up from the coffee table and texted a message. "Micah says to leave it out of your phone but not to destroy it. That way she will come to them and they can be ready for her."

"So, she knows where I am."

"I don't want to lie to you. Yes, chances are that she knows exactly where you are."

The thought appalled her. She felt her stomach roll over, and Amelia thought she might throw up.

"Hey," he said and cupped her face. "I've got you."

Those three words were like a gift from heaven. No one had made her feel as protected in her whole life. And for a moment her whole being and soul seemed to put the terror that had been going through her to the back of her mind.

She opened her mouth to say something, but there were no words. She knew what he was going to do before he did it…kiss her. She waited for the feel of his lips on hers. Liam tipped her chin up, and she contemplated kissing him first, but somehow, she found her nerve gave out at the last second. The touch of his fingers as his thumb smoothed the skin on her cheek somehow made her feel problem-free…just for that moment.

"Thank you for being with me, helping in this impossible situation that has nothing to do with you, and yet here you are."

"My pleasure," he said in a husky, deep tone. Even with those few words, his voice was mesmerizing. "We should eat. I was chopping a salad when you came down."

"I'm not hungry," she said.

"Me neither."

Oh Lord, she hadn't been with a man in a very long time. It wasn't something that had been at the front of her mind. *Once bitten, twice shy* had been her motto. Tony had totally ruined any trust she'd had.

Life was far more uncomplicated and safe on her own. She wasn't responsible for anyone else, she hadn't had to fret about anyone's safety or security…only had herself to worry about.

She had tried so hard not to become involved with Liam. And yet here she was, sitting next to him, waiting for those wide, well-shaped lips to touch hers. The moment was so tense that she could have literally cut the air with a knife.

Was that her heart thumping so loudly?

"No," he said, "It's mine." And he took her hand and

laid it on his chest.

"Did I say that out loud?"

He nodded.

She could feel the *thud*, *thud*, *thud* of his heartbeat beneath his shirt.

****

Liam knew that Amelia wanted to shut him out. He was well aware that if she could, she would take off into the night. Her physical effect on his senses was overwhelming, but it was nothing compared to the emotional impact she was having on him.

It would be far easier if it was just sexual desire, but it was that and all of the above. Liam wanted her so much that he could feel himself shaking with the need for her in every aspect, and he'd never felt like that before.

He shouldn't be doing this. She'd been through enough. But those eyes were staring back at him with hope, and he wasn't sure he could live up to the expectations of that desire. Her skin was pale, and she looked exhausted. But he did not doubt that she had strength. No one went through what she had without fighting.

From the very first moment he'd seen her, Liam was absolutely sure that she was going to be special in his life. How did that happen? How can you just look at a person and know that you want to spend the rest of your life with them?

There was a peacefulness around them, nothing like the unyielding violence that had dogged them. Her hair was still drying after her shower, and it flowed in curls over her shoulder and down over her breasts.

She blinked her eyes. "Thank you for taking such good care of me, Liam."

The acceleration of his pulse at the sound of his name on her lips left him breathless, and he caught whiffs of the scent of her shampoo. The smell of coconut and vanilla flowed over his senses, and he wanted to bury his lips in her locks.

"It isn't needed," he said.

She tentatively smiled, and a rush of pink stained her cheeks. "It is, this is a massive thing you are doing."

"Maybe, but I want to help you as much as I can." He wanted to claim her as his, which was a very neanderthal feeling, but he couldn't help it.

He leaned in until he could feel her breath on his lips. Liam wanted to give her a chance to say no. But thank God she didn't, and he softly kissed her. It was like an explosion of fireworks. He could feel her trembling. She opened her mouth more, her tongue touching his, and Liam gave up any hope of going slowly with her.

Amelia moved closer to him, her hands pressed against his chest, and he wanted to groan aloud at the sensual contact. Her sexy lips parted. Liam moved his hands up and down her arms, and as he did, his thumb felt the hardness of her nipple as it protruded through her t-shirt.

"Oh God," he groaned. This was getting out of hand way too quickly, and he didn't want fast. He wanted slow so that he could enjoy every single bit of her.

She gasped out a breath as he let his mouth work its way down the silky skin of her neck.

"Liam," she whispered lightly in his ear.

Emotion stirred through his body, and his voice shook as he whispered, "Yes."

"It's been a long time since I did this."

"I should let you rest. I should give you time to think

about us."

"Us?"

He took hold of her hands and turned them face up before leaning in to kiss each one. The pounding of her pulse thumped against his lips.

"I've never hidden how I feel about you. Those feelings have just gotten more and more intensified."

To his surprise, she nodded. "Me too, but I'm so worried about what being with me will do to you."

"Honey, I'm a big boy, and I'm prepared to protect you any way I have to."

She clutched at his shoulders, drawing him down to her. She lay back against the cushions, lifting her legs onto the sofa, and he followed suit, lying beside her, face to face, heart to heart. Just for one single moment, he felt her curves all soft next to him and he pulled her closer.

It took but a second for their lips to meet in a kiss so sweet it took his breath away, before a bolt of lightning surged through him from head to toe. The feel of her body as they touched skin-to-skin was powerfully consuming. Even her heartbeat pulsed strongly next to his.

When they broke apart, there was a surprised look on her face. They were both breathing heavily.

"Amelia...Milly." His voice was low and gruff even to his own ears.

"I like it when you say my name, you sound husky." She stared at him from beneath her long, dark lashes. "Sexy." The salacious word was breathlessly said. Then, as if embarrassed, she buried her face into his neck and her lips pressed a kiss there.

Oh, fuck!

He knew that being with him was beginning to mean

something to her. She didn't trust easily, and he wondered how long it had been since she'd been with a man. He admired her strength and the way her loyalty meant more to her than her own safety.

Just being with her gave him the sense that he could do anything he wanted to, and no one had ever made him feel that way. He shouldn't let this happen, he really shouldn't. There was so much going on. But he couldn't bring himself to put a stop to his rampant emotions.

When she lifted her face, he couldn't stop himself from leaning in closer and kissing her. She groaned, which sent a zing right down to the bulge behind the zipper on his jeans. Liam opened his mouth wider on hers and let her lead the way. He wanted it to be her choice where this kiss would lead.

"Beautiful," he whispered.

She kissed him back with zest and passion, and his heart was pounding way harder than it ever had before. His hands skimmed up and down her back, drawing her closer at the same time. She arched into him, pressing against him as she sought more of his body. The more he roused her passion, the stronger his got.

The reality of it was that he'd been fantasizing about her since they first met, but real life was far better than anything he'd ever dreamed. Liam should have said no, but he didn't want to, because this woman was beginning to—no, not *beginning*…she was *definitely* going to be a massive part of his life.

But hadn't he known that from the outset!

****

He had called her beautiful. Amelia's heart did a summersault at the endearment. Every woman liked to be told that, but the way he said it made her melt into a puddle of wanton desire.

She knew Liam would never do anything to hurt her. Right from the beginning, he'd shown her that he was interested. He had never hidden that, but there had been no pushing her to do anything she wasn't happy to do.

"I trust you," she said against his lips. She felt herself blush when he looked at her with one eyebrow quirked.

"Good to know."

"I mean…you know…" she stammered like a teenager.

He smiled. "It's okay, I know what you mean, and I love that you feel like that."

She should have known he would understand. He always seemed to, as if he knew her as well as she knew herself.

"Amelia?"

"Umm," she murmured.

"How long since you were last with a man?"

Shit! She drew her face back from where he was caressing her lips.

"Hey." A smile creased his face. "It doesn't matter. You don't have to tell me. Just be comfortable with how you feel, okay?"

Her cheeks felt hot, and she knew they were as red as molten lava. His lips brushed the heat.

Amelia swallowed. "A few years. More than a few actually," she said, lowering her head.

Liam pushed his fingers through her hair and lifted her face so that she was staring right into his eyes. He drew in a deep, audible breath, the surprise evident in his expression.

"We can take this as slow as you like," he said, his

breath fanning her cheeks.

She was breathing quickly, not sure what he was going to say. She was relieved when he didn't laugh at her inexperience, but she somehow knew Liam would never do that. Amelia felt as though she was floating on a cloud.

She pressed her mouth against his. "I don't want to take it slow…I need you now."

"I feel the same way." He kissed her with an urgency that she returned with vigor, leaving her in no doubt about him and what she wanted.

"Shall we take this upstairs?" he asked as they broke their kiss for air.

Amelia nodded, and he stood up, pulling her up with him.

"Just let me set the alarm and check all the doors." He leaned down and gave her a quick kiss. "God, I could stand here and stare at you all night." His dark gaze settled on hers, and he squeezed her hands before letting them go. "I won't be long."

She watched him go around checking the doors and windows. Amelia stretched her arms above her head, getting out all the kinks. Misty meowed at her but seemed okay. She went over to where she was curled up by the window and stroked her head.

The drapes were pulled back, and she wondered if she should close them. There was a full moon outside, and it spread its light onto the darkness of the night. As she gazed out the window, she realized that anyone could be out there now, right this minute looking back at her, and she wouldn't know.

She shivered and tried to control the sense of fear that skittered down her spine. Amelia felt safe here with

Liam, but not knowing what was going to happen made her feel very protective toward him. He had no idea what kind of family he was dealing with, but she did…only too well.

"Let's close these," he said as he stood behind her doing just that. Turning her around, he took her hand.

"Are all the doors locked?"

He nodded. "Yes, and the windows too. The alarm is set, so if anyone comes as far as the perimeter of the house, then I'll get a notification on my phone, which in turn will notify the sheriff. The security team I've hired will be here in the morning," Liam said as he drew her to his side, putting an arm around her shoulders.

Leaning down, he picked up his cell from the coffee table and shoved it into his jeans pocket.

"Come on, let's go to bed." He guided her to the stairs, and they climbed them in silence.

Holy cow, her heart raced at a hundred miles per hour, which made her completely breathless.

They reached her bedroom door, but he didn't open it, instead he looked at her as she lifted her head.

"You can change your mind at any point." He deliberately turned her to face him and scrutinized her carefully, his stare intense as it swept over her.

Amelia couldn't explain why, but she had no nerves at all. The last two days had made her realize that she had been dreaming if she ever thought she'd be safe. Liam, in the short while she had known him, made her feel safe for the first time in so, so long.

It was a humongous surprise to her, one that didn't make any sense, but sometimes the best things in life didn't, and you either picked it to bits or you went with that new feeling; she chose the latter. As he stood opposite her, waiting patiently for her to decide, she knew that there was no decision necessary; it had been a *yes* from the word *go*.

They had no past, no little connections that made a relationship, but somehow they both seemed to know that this was right…they were right. As she looked up at him, his brown hair was streaked with the sun, probably a little longer than when she'd first met him. She decided she liked the way he hadn't shaved, and she was dying to touch his stubbled cheeks…so she did, cupping his jaw in her hand.

He leaned into her palm but still didn't do anything, waiting for her permission. It was kinda cute and old-fashioned, which was just another thing she liked about him. Sometimes one just knew what was right. At that moment he was what she wanted, and there was no doubt in her mind about that.

"I don't want to change my mind," she said with a smile. "But it's been so long since I—"

He touched his fingers to her mouth so she couldn't say anything else. "It doesn't matter. It's here and now that is most important."

Liam took her hand and tugged her down the hall to the other side of the house to what she assumed would be his bedroom. Seconds later they were inside his room, and he closed the door behind him.

The sound of silence was only introjected by their breathing. How was it that she knew this was going to be one of those moments she would never forget? Facing him, her body shivered at the pleasure she knew she was going to have, certain it would be far more than she'd ever experienced.

Her thoughts were broken by the feel of his lips on

hers, his tongue slick as he gently drew her lower lip between his teeth, nibbling at the skin. Who knew that would be so sensuous?

In the short time they had known each other they had hardly kissed at all, but holy cow, it was one of the most pleasurable kisses she'd ever experienced. At this moment, tonight, she would take the time to get to know this man, learn what pleasured him and how they could connect in this act of sheer indulgence between a man and a woman.

Her hands lay on his chest, and when she used her tongue to lick his lips she could feel his muscles beneath her fingers jump. She took great satisfaction in knowing she could do that to him.

From then on he let her lead with the kiss. He was such a big man, both in height and presence, and she guessed the latter came from being in court. She wanted to taste him so much more, and as all these thoughts were jumping around in her mind, she used her teeth to nibble at his jawline. His earlobe was her next destination, and the prickle of his growth felt strangely good. As she slid her hands up his chest and around his neck he pulled her even closer, his arms wrapped tightly around her. Their hips were pressed together, and she could feel how aroused he was.

Suddenly, Liam lifted her, and she laughed as she wrapped her legs around his hips. His hands held onto her ass as he moved over to the bed. Amelia only had eyes for him, nothing else could have drawn her away from his gaze. He kissed her hard before letting her drop gently in front of him.

"I want you naked," he said hoarsely.

Amelia was breathing so fast that she couldn't get

any words out, so she just lifted the hem of her t-shirt and drew it over her head.

He did the same, and she was oxygen deprived. He was quite simply gorgeous. Who knew what he had been hiding beneath his clothes? Hard, tanned abs stared back at her, and she wanted to kiss each and every one.

She just had a plain, black bra on, but he didn't seem to mind, because his gaze took on a glazed look, and she knew it wouldn't have mattered what she was wearing.

He leaned down and kissed the top of each of her breasts. It was wonderful, so gentle and yet with a promise of things to come. He reached around and undid her bra—oh, what a glorious feeling it was—and when his lips touched the hardness of her nipple she thought she was going to explode.

"Liam," she whispered. "That feels so good."

And it did. He somehow made her feel like his lips were massaging her breasts. It was sexy, sultry, and downright orgasmic. She couldn't help but arch her back, encouraging him to do more of what he was already treating her to.

"I want you, so much," he said as he kissed her, devouring everything she had to offer him.

Using both hands, he cupped her breasts and buried his face in them, opening his mouth to the small globes as if they were something he couldn't bear to be parted from.

Liam paused and lifted his dark gaze to hers. She brushed his hair back, her fingertips lightly digging into his scalp. She drew her other hand down his taut stomach to the buckle of his jeans and started to undo it.

"No," he said, covering her hand. "If you do that, this will be over far quicker than I want it to."

"Jeez, Liam, I want quick. I want you. It's been so, so long since I felt a man's hands on me."

He looked momentarily surprised. "So the mouse is, in fact, a lion." He chuckled. "I like that. I like you," he said with sincerity etched over his face.

Amelia swallowed. Oh hell!

He undid her jeans, and she stepped out of them as he kneeled in front of her. Touching the front of her panties, he groaned. "You're wet," he said.

She was.

Her heartbeat raced as fast as a lightning strike when he put his lips there, and if he hadn't had hold of her, she would have fallen to the floor.

"So damn sweet," he said as he licked the inside of her thigh.

"Oh God." He was going to kill her with that mouth. "Liam, I want to touch you."

He looked up at her, and there was sheer, unadulterated desire in those beautiful eyes. They had turned navy blue, so intense, so damned sexy.

"You can, but at this moment it's all about you."

Oh hell!

His fingers slipped into the side of her panties. "These have to go," he said, slowly dragging them down her legs.

His jaw grazed over her skin as his tongue made her think of all the wicked things she wanted him to do. Her knees were wobbling big time. He gripped hold of her hips, holding her while he softly and painstakingly drove her wild. Her hips jerked uncontrollably. It was torture, but in a good way. She wanted him inside her so much.

"Please," she begged.

But he didn't stop. His mouth ravished her wet flesh.

153

"Liam." She'd never heard such urgency in her voice before.

She had her fingers in his hair, and she was pulling it tight. She knew it must have hurt, but she couldn't help it. He was driving her insane, the wild pleasure leaving her on the precipice of something magnificent. His hot, laving tongue explored her whole body, keeping her a prisoner of his desire as she trembled in a mass of anticipation. And when she could stand it no more, he took her over the edge.

"Oh…oh…oh!" Her voice rose higher and higher until, breathless, she couldn't speak at all. Her eyes fluttered open, and Liam caught her in his arms and lay her on the bed.

Good God, am I still alive?

Chapter 9

Liam barely stopped himself from saying those three little words...*I Love You*. He wasn't sure if Amelia was ready to hear them yet. Fuck, he had only just managed to wrap his head around the fact that he had fallen for this woman so damned quickly.

How did he know that she was the one? That was a question he couldn't answer because he just did.

Watching her come all over his hand was the most mesmeric, the sexiest, heart-skipping moment he'd ever experienced. She'd gone so long without sex, but boy she'd shown him just how much she wanted him.

Acquiescence filled her features, and it made him feel kinda good to know that he had given her the satisfaction, although how the hell he was controlling himself was beyond his imagination.

Taking his jeans off, he reached into his pocket and removed his wallet before dropping them to the floor. Thankfully, inside were two condoms, which had been there a while. He took them out, then tossed his wallet on top of his clothes. He quickly covered himself before crawling over her. The feel of her naked body beneath his was enough to make him groan out loud. Fuck, she felt so good; so, so good.

She clutched at his shoulders. "Liam." Her voice shook.

As he bent down and pressed his lips onto hers, the

intensity of the kiss almost blew his mind, and she returned his fervor. They were a perfect fit. He could feel her soft, silky thighs cradling his hips. He had this uncontrollable need for her, and it wasn't just the sex. It was being near her. With her. Watching her.

Her breasts were cushioned beneath his chest. His own nipples were pressed into hers, and fuck if that wasn't a turn on all by itself. Amelia locked her arms around his neck at the same time she wrapped her legs around him, the heels of her feet digging into the small of his back.

"Is this okay?" she asked.

Liam closed his eyes for a moment, trying to discipline himself to go slow. It had been a long time since she'd last been with a man, and he didn't want to hurt her. He could feel her wetness against him, so hot, and she lifted her hips, urging him to take her.

He was on his elbows, and he grabbed hold of one of the pillows.

"Lift your hips," he said. When she did as he requested, he slipped the pillow beneath her. "This will help. I don't want to hurt you."

"Oh, Liam, you would never hurt me. I know that, and I trust you."

"Okay…" He partially slipped into her; slow was killing him.

He felt her tense, and he looked at her. Her eyes were closed, but when she opened them he could see the desire in their depths. She held him captive with the passion glazing them. Thankfully, he could see no pain reflected in those beautiful eyes.

"If I hurt you, you tell me, okay?"

She nodded. "I will, but you're hurting me more by

going so slow. I'm not made of china, I won't break."

He couldn't stop the groan that elicited inside him. He thrust in, and despite what she said, he went slowly until he could bury himself no more. She was so tight, so silky. God, he was trembling. He withdrew and thrust in again, and again, and again.

Amelia was holding on to him tightly, making sounds of pleasure. She was flushed, and her eyes glittered. He could see that she was almost there. All it took was a few more thrusts and she tightened around him. It felt so fucking good.

"Oh God," she breathed out. "Yes," she said. "Harder, Liam, harder…please."

He obliged, and she took him with her as she arched into his body, her head thrown back as he was drained of everything he had in the most mind-blowing orgasm. She pressed into him for a few moments more until she went utterly limp beneath him.

Liam didn't want to move. He liked the feeling of being inside her. They were both struggling to breathe. He leaned down and brushed his lips over hers. He found that to him she was irresistible, and the moment between them had been more than he ever thought it could be. His heartbeat pounded, echoing hers.

"Thank you," she said.

"For what?" he asked, frowning.

"For not giving up on me." She squeezed his shoulder.

"Never." He loved how husky her voice was, and he covered her mouth with his own. "I should move. I'm way too heavy to be laying on top of you like this."

"No." She stopped him from moving by gripping him tightly. "Just a few moments more, please."

He realized that she was still having tiny contractions, and he felt her muscles squeeze tightly over him. Her breathing was labored, and her fingers scraped over his ass. God, he was going to get hard again. Lifting his head, he looked at the ethereal expression on her face. Her gaze shimmered with desire.

"I can't help it," she said. "I want you." Her murmur was so soft and sexy.

He was still buried inside her, and he wanted to make love to her again. He swallowed her whimper with his mouth and let her ride her way through the tiny contractions until she stilled.

"Are you okay?" he asked her.

Looking straight into his eyes, she nodded. "Yes. I'm more than okay," she said with a smile spreading over her face.

He brushed a strand of hair from her face and pressed his lips to her forehead before leaving her to go to the bathroom. When he returned to the bedroom she was fast asleep, and it made him smile. Climbing back into bed, he wrapped her up close to him and listened to her steady breathing.

He would protect Amelia with his life if necessary. There was no way he was going to let anyone hurt her. How on earth did it make sense for him to feel like that? His attraction to her had been instant, the chemistry was there from the beginning.

Liam would take no chances. He couldn't handle losing her. It wasn't even something he wanted to think about. And with that thought, he felt his eyes get heavy. It had been a long few days, and he hadn't realized how tired he was.

****

Liam scrubbed a hand over his eyes as his cell buzzed. He felt for it on the nightstand but remembered it was still in his jeans pocket. Amelia was still fast asleep, wrapped up in his arms, and he gently removed himself from the bed.

Swiping on the screen, he saw that it was an alert letting him know that someone was coming up the driveway. He quickly picked up his clothes from the floor and slipped on his jeans and t-shirt as he opened the door and walked out of the bedroom.

He knew that if it was Max or Jarrod they would have texted him first. Hurrying down the staircase, he went over to the window by the front door and drew the curtain aside to see who it was.

A large, black SUV pulled up to the front of the house. The windows were tinted, and he didn't recognize it.

Shit!

His weapon was locked away in the safe. He'd meant to get it out earlier, but he'd been a little distracted by Amelia. He was just about to call the local sheriff when his friend Micah King exited the vehicle along with his passenger, whom Liam didn't recognize.

He didn't mind admitting that he was glad to see him. Micah was dressed in a dark suit. The other guy wore jeans and a leather jacket. Both of the men had on aviator sunglasses.

Micah was a former marine and Navy SEAL, and he was very good at what he did. He was also a straight-up guy, and he took every job that his team did very seriously, which was one of the reasons he was the best.

Liam trusted him, and he'd worked with him many times, especially when he'd been doing high-profile cases. He turned off the alarm and then opened the door, stepping out to meet the men.

"Hey, Micah. Thanks for this." Liam reached out and shook the man's hand.

"It's not a problem, Liam. I'm just sorry that this is happening."

Liam scrubbed his hand over his face. "You and me both, buddy," he muttered as the other man came up to stand by Micah.

"This is one of my new employees, Griffin Reed."

They shook hands; he had a firm handshake. "Nice place you have here," he said.

Liam didn't feel like explaining that he didn't own it, and it wasn't really relevant information anyway. "Come in, I'll put some coffee on," he said, turning to head back into the house.

They entered the house and shut the door. Liam turned the alarm back on.

"That's a pretty sophisticated alarm you have there," Micah said as Liam finished punching the numbers in.

He nodded. "It seemed appropriate after all the hard work we've done and the fact that the cabin isn't occupied all the time."

The two men followed him into the kitchen. He put the coffee on and then turned to face them and explained everything that had happened.

"Why has Amelia not gone into WISTEC?" Griffin asked him. "It would be the safest thing to do, and we could still take care of her."

Liam shook his head. "Honestly, I think it's gone too far, and also, she's fed up with running. Living in Cape Charles for so long made her feel comfortable, and if after six years she's not going to be safe, then we have to face it."

Liam went to pick up the small tracker that he'd found in her phone and handed it to Micah.

"What are you going to do with that?" he asked as the man took it from him.

"Exactly nothing," he said, putting it down on the countertop. "Let's see how long it takes this woman to get here."

Liam nodded. He didn't like the sound of it, but he knew it was probably the only way to end this. "I'll go get Amelia," Liam said once he'd set a cup of coffee in front of each of the men.

Climbing the stairs two at a time, he headed for his bedroom. Opening the door, he saw that she was already up and dressed, sitting on the edge of the bed. There was a worried look on her face, and she looked tense—really tense—as she clasped her hands together.

"Is everything okay?" she whispered, her voice barely audible.

He nodded as he went to sit beside her. She had light blue jeans on with a halter neck top in dark blue. He wasn't exactly sure how he felt about anyone seeing her looking so beautiful and sexy.

"My friend with the security business is here," he said as he took hold of her hand and kissed her fingers.

Turning so that she was facing him, she looked as though she was thinking about what she wanted to say.

"I'm so sorry, Liam, for bringing all this trouble to your doorstep."

"Enough, there's no need. This isn't your fault. Just for doing the right thing the Rossi family has made your life a living misery. Well, that stops right here, and I want to help, so let me. Please."

She belonged wherever he was, not on the run, and certainly never frightened for her life the way this woman was making Amelia feel.

"Come on," he said. "Let's go over what we're going to do and see if we can catch this nasty piece of work."

There was a hesitation in her eyes. "Promise me you won't do anything stupid?" she said.

"I don't intend to, sweetheart." And he smiled at her, not really knowing what was about to happen. But knowing that if it came to it, he would protect her in any way he had to.

****

Ivy Rossi surveyed the red light she'd been watching on her phone. It had been in one spot for quite some time. She'd been observing the house for the last five hours. It was going to be hard to access. Only one way in and out, and she'd seen a black SUV go up the drive. It could have been the feds, she couldn't tell.

It was almost impossible to keep her son informed of what she was doing. Tony wasn't as fiery as Angus, but where had that gotten him? In prison because of the bitch inside that house. If it hadn't been for Amelia, both of Ivy's sons would have been with her, and Angus would have been the head of the family business.

She was hot as she sat in an old car that had no AC. Either that or she was having hot flashes. After the mistake she'd made setting off the car bomb too early, she wanted to make absolutely certain she got it right this time. Perhaps she'd torture Amelia a little before she killed her.

Ivy smiled at the thought. It gave her a thrill to think about doing that. What she could do with a knife was way more than her sons knew. And she'd managed to find a spot where she couldn't be detected. She could hardly contain her excitement.

Ivy leaned down and checked the gun in her bag. It was all ready for everything she had planned, and the long, sharp knife was a particular favorite from her younger days when she used to be a contracted assassin for anyone who would pay her enough.

That was how she'd met her husband. He was head of one of the most influential families in the east end of London. When he spoke, people listened, until a sniper from another family took him out. Angus got revenge, but he was paying the price now.

Once she saw the SUV leave she would set up her cell jammer. It had the ability to block reception for up to ten phones up to a hundred meters.

She could see the windows from her binoculars, but she had yet to see any sign of Amelia. The bitch was hiding behind her new man. But she would have to come out at some point, and Ivy was ready for her. And this time she would not miss.

She checked to make sure the gun was loaded, then smiled as she attached the silencer on it. No one would hear a thing until it was too late.

****

Amelia followed Liam downstairs, and he introduced her to the two men. The one in the suit, Micah, looked formidable. She could see that this man did not suffer fools gladly. He had an air of confidence about him. He was in charge, and no one would doubt that. The other one, Griffin, seemed more laid-back, but she could see mystery in his eyes. He was younger than Micah but looked as if he knew how to handle himself.

163

Both men were very good-looking, and for some reason she trusted them, and that didn't happen often to her. These men were putting their lives at risk for her, and Liam was paying them to do it. She didn't even want to know how much it was costing him.

"Everything is going to be fine." Micah smiled at her as she sat at the breakfast bar while Liam stood at her side. "We will catch the perpetrator, but you have to do as we ask. From what Liam has told me, I know that's going to be hard for you, but be assured we know what we're doing."

"If Liam trusts you, then so do I," she muttered, not being able to return the smile because of the fear inside her.

How could she live with herself if something happened to someone who was trying to keep her safe? What if Liam got hurt…or worse. She shivered, although she wasn't cold.

"Are you all right?" Liam squeezed her shoulder, and she looked up at him.

"Yes. How can I not be with you all looking out for me?"

After that, there was a lot of coming and going by the two men. They installed several cameras that gave an overall view of the property. There were lots of discussions and plans to catch Ivy if she came near. Well, it wasn't *if* but *when*, because they all knew that day was coming.

Amelia was terrified, but she just wanted the whole scenario to be over. Her nerves were a wreck, and the worry that someone would get hurt was chilling her insides. She was tense and on edge all the time.

The marshals would be there in the morning, more

people to watch over her. She felt as if her life was on a turntable and she was right back to when she was waiting to go to court eight years ago.

It was a long day, and by early evening she was exhausted. Micah and Griffin had just left to be replaced by two others. Liam chatted with them while she went upstairs to take a hot shower.

Reveling in the heat, Amelia closed her eyes and lifted her head up so the water ran over her face, neck, and body. She felt as if she was washing away Ivy, for a few minutes anyway.

She nearly had a heart attack when the glass door opened.

"Need some company?"

She didn't even have to think about that. "Yes."

He stripped naked and walked in, shutting the door behind himself.

"Help me forget," she said.

"With pleasure," he muttered.

He leaned down and kissed her slow and thoroughly, his hands touching her ass, massaging the flesh. Amelia didn't need an invitation to stroke the strong muscles on Liam's back. Every muscle shuddered as her fingers traced his smooth skin.

He stopped kissing her, and she saw the dark fire in the depths of his eyes. Amelia dug her nails in. He made a sound of unadulterated male pleasure when their naked thighs rubbed together, and she could feel the desire kindle between her legs.

The myriad of sensations that were running through her body made her heart thump wildly, and when he lifted her she didn't think twice about wrapping her legs around him. He raised his mouth from her lips and smiled at her—a gentle smile. She saw not just desire, but a warmth.

"Once they find Ivy Rossi and that part of your life is put to rest, we can concentrate on us then."

Was he talking about a future together? His hand rhythmically stroked her hip. Water poured over them, and her core was pressing against his hardness, but he seemed to be waiting for an answer from her, and she honestly didn't know what to say

She knew that her feelings for him were turning into love, but how could she plan for a future when she didn't even know if she had one?

"Let's just see what happens," she said. Her stomach gave a twist of apprehension as she spoke the words.

"Did you love Tony?" An emotion she didn't recognize flashed in his eyes.

Her memory went back to those first days they were together, before she found out who he was.

"I guess I thought I was in love, thought that he loved me, but that turned out to be wrong." Her time with Tony Rossi, combined with what occurred afterward, not only changed her life forever but made her grow up very quickly.

He nuzzled her neck. "This isn't wrong," he said. "You and I are going to be a lot more."

She moved her head to one side as his lips made the journey from her jawline to her hardened nipple. The guy was seriously strong as he held her as if she weighed nothing at all.

She tried to focus on what he'd said, but his lips were driving her crazy, and she couldn't concentrate. The way his teeth nibbled her hardened skin made her groan out loud, her breathing rapid.

"The very first time I saw you, I wanted you," he said, cupping her face.

He kissed her, and it was full of promise, and in turn, she could feel the heavenly shivers run down her spine, even though the water was steaming hot. The lubricant of the hot water was sensual as he smoothed his hands over her ass, his hand gripping the flesh.

Amelia couldn't help the small assenting moans coming from her mouth. Her womb was tightening, and she wanted him inside her, but he continued to tease her with those luscious lips.

She arched her body, pressing against him, encouraging them to take this further. His ardor suddenly increased, and she responded with as much passion as him. Without warning, he stopped and leaned his forehead on hers, breathing really fast.

"What's wrong?" she asked.

"Condom."

"Do you have one?" *Please say yes*, she thought with a little desperation.

"One left." He let her down. "Don't move," he said, giving her a quick kiss on the lips before opening the door and stepping out.

She leaned back against the tiled wall, the cold shocking her for a moment, but it did nothing to cool down her ardor. She'd never wanted anyone as much as she did him. The way they made love was like a well-oiled machine.

In a space of days, she felt more for this man than she ever thought was possible. Was it love? God, she just needed to end the drama in her life once and for all. And she knew a way to do it without anyone else getting hurt. It was the only way.

Liam came back, and just for this moment she forgot about anything else that was going on; she just wanted the here and now. He'd put the condom on, and she wrapped her arms and legs around him as he lifted her up and hugged her to him.

Their passion was instant, and her ankles locked around his waist. Liam groaned as he slid inside her, deep. He pulled out, almost completely, then thrust in hard again.

"God, you're so sexy," he said, his voice low and husky as if he could hardly get the words out.

He began a rhythm, and she tried to move her hips faster, but he was controlling the movements. He kissed her, his tongue wreaking havoc in her mouth. The intensity of the moment was almost too much to bear.

Then she felt those internal contractions that were bringing her closer to the edge.

"Liam, Liam," she said against his mouth.

"Are you ready?" he groaned out.

"God, yes. Now, Liam, now." She was almost shouting at him, trying to keep her need under control.

He pressed his face into her neck and gave into her. They both groaned out loud, and it was like a detonation of passion and desire spilling over her skin, joining him to her in a way that was going to be hard to shake.

This was more than just a few nights of passion; this was love…she loved him. And it made her more determined to do what she now knew she had to. There was no other way to end the nightmare that had plagued her for years.

Chapter 10

Liam stretched before he opened his eyes. He felt good. He and Amelia had shared another special moment in the shower. When they'd gone to bed she had snuggled up close to him and he had wrapped her tightly in his arms.

As he turned his head it was to see that the only indication that Amelia had been there was the indentation of her head on the pillow. Apparently, she had already gotten up. He lifted his wrist to look at his watch. A quarter after seven; slightly later than he was used to getting up in the morning.

Pushing the covers back, he got out of bed and slipped his jeans on. Opening the top drawer of the dresser, he took out a t-shirt and slipped it on as he walked to the door. He padded barefoot downstairs, expecting to find her in the kitchen, but there was no evidence of her.

He went to the small room where the security team had set up their equipment, and he saw that Micah and Griffin had returned.

"Morning, guys. Has anyone seen Amelia?"

Micah looked at him before he stood up. "No. Is she not with you?"

Liam shook his head. "No."

He went back out and opened the front door.

"Amelia," Liam yelled, but there was no response.

"Shit," he mumbled.

When he stepped back inside, Micah was already on the phone and Griffin was checking his gun before putting it in the waistband of his jeans.

"Don't worry, we'll find her," Griffin said before stepping outside and shutting the door behind him.

"What the fuck, Micah? How the hell did she get out without you seeing her?" he said irritably to his friend.

"No one has had eyes on her," he said once he'd put the phone back in his pocket.

"Shit. I thought there were cameras everywhere?" Liam said, his voice teetering on shouting.

"There are!"

"Fuck!"

"Has she left a note?" Micah asked him.

A note. His eyes scanned everywhere, and he saw something on the kitchen counter. Striding over there, he picked up the folded piece of paper that had his name on it. He was almost too frightened to open it, but he did. His eyes skimmed the words.

Liam,

I can't just sit around and wait for Ivy to do something that might hurt you. I couldn't bear that. It would break my heart.

Trust me, this is the only way.

I didn't realize until last night how easy it was to fall in love with you. You've protected me so well, and I know you would put me before you. I won't let that happen.

Please look after Misty for me.

Amelia xx

He tossed the note on the counter, and Micah picked it up and read it. His mind turned over the words Amelia had written. She thought she was saving him, but without her he was nothing.

"Where's the tracker?" Micah asked.

Liam scanned the countertop as realization dawned on him. Amelia had taken it…she was trying to draw Ivy Rossi to her. *Holy fuck!*

Liam's jaw clenched, and his fist crashed down on the counter. "Damn it. Micah, where the hell is she?"

At that moment Griffin came back in, and they both looked up expectantly.

"Anything?" Micah asked Griffin.

"She cut a hole in the east side fence. There is a two-foot hidden spot from our cameras. It's very crafty how she knew where that was."

"What do you mean?" Liam asked.

Micah replied, "She was watching us set up yesterday. Remember she has been hiding very well for the past eight years."

Micah got on his phone again, and Liam sat down, absolutely devastated. Misty jumped on his knee. "Hey, buddy," he said as he stroked the soft fur. "Where is she?"

The cat meowed at him as if to say *get off your ass and find my mommy*.

He stood up. "When are the marshals going to be here?"

"They should arrive any time now," Griffin answered as Liam followed both of them into the makeshift security room.

"Let's run the tape back," Micah said.

As Liam stood back, watching the three screens, his heart was beating so fast he could barely catch his breath.

"There," he said as he saw Amelia with a rucksack on her back. She had a hat on which covered her face, but he knew it was her.

As the tape was stopped Liam stared at her on the screen. God, she could be anywhere now.

"One good thing about her taking the tracker is that as soon as she puts it into her phone, we will be able to identify where she is." Micah tapped away at something on his phone, then looked up at Griffin. "Okay, let's work the perimeter before we go further afield. You take the east side and I'll take the west and work in a clockwise formation." Micah put his hand on Liam's shoulder. "We'll find her. You stay here in case she comes back."

"Not a fucking chance. I'm not going to sit around here just waiting, I'm coming with you," Liam replied firmly.

"I don't suppose there's anything I can say to stop you?"

"What do you think?"

"Okay, you stay with me."

He couldn't ever remember being so frightened, not for himself but the thought of losing her was tearing him apart. A cold tremor raced through his body as he realized the possibility of not finding Amelia could be very real.

****

Amelia had been walking for half a day. She had no idea where she was, but she had kept away from the main roads. She sat on a rock, trying to identify her surroundings. The ski resort was just ahead of her now, but she didn't want to go there, too many people.

Setting her rucksack down, she opened it and took a bottle of water out. This bag had been packed for years just in case an occasion like this ever arose. There was money, her passport, snacks, a map, and some clothes. Just the essentials; no more, no less.

She'd hoped never to have to use it, but when she'd packed it in her suitcase to travel with Liam, she'd had a feeling that things were going to go wrong and she'd need it. Amelia felt a panic like she'd never known before well up in her throat.

She'd always had a plan, but that was from her home in Cape Charles. Here, she knew nothing about the landscape, and had no idea where there were any safe spots for her to hide.

There was silence everywhere, and she was surrounded by trees. The map she had didn't cover this area. Taking her cell out, she tried to get reception so that she could get the navigation system working.

Standing up, she moved around, holding the phone in the air. "Shit," she muttered under her breath. There was nothing, not even one bar. She became more uncomfortable by the minute.

Amelia had hated leaving Liam. It had broken her heart, but it was the only way to keep him safe. She imagined him waking up and finding her note. He would blame the security team, but it wasn't their fault.

Noticing the space that the cameras didn't cover had been a fluke on her part. It was only when she realized she'd gotten away undetected that she knew they hadn't covered the small area she had crawled out of.

She bit her lip as she sat down, putting her water back in her rucksack. Scrubbing her fingers through her hair, she understood how alone she was; it didn't matter how long she had been like this, it never got any easier.

Amelia steadied the phone on her knee as she took the back off and drew out the tracker from her pocket that she'd taken with her before leaving the cabin. She looked at it in between her thumb and forefinger. It was amazing to think that someone could find out where you were with something so small.

Breathing in deep, she put it back inside her phone where Liam had taken it from, totally aware that by doing so she was putting herself in extreme danger. It would pull Ivy away from the cabin and toward her. When she had put the case back on, she tucked the phone into her pocket.

Now let's see what happens next.

The sun was rising, so Amelia headed toward it, using that as a point of guidance. She was no expert at navigation, but she knew that in the US the sun rose in the east. Beech Mountain was one of the higher peaks of the Blue Ridge Mountains range, so she headed toward that. If she was perfectly honest, her skills were not the best at directions.

The air was cool, and the sounds of birds shrieking were scaring the crap out of her. The forest was thick with growth, and the trees were gently swaying. The leaves were rustling, and occasionally she smelled a sweet, floral scent.

She followed a path that had quite clearly been made over time, so at least she knew other people had been before her and she was on a track to somewhere. It felt completely terrifying to know she'd set herself up as bait, to lure evil away from the man she loved.

Amelia hated the heavy heart that settled against her ribs. This was why she had refused to get close to people. Even Lizzie, who was her friend, had been kept at a distance, and Amelia had felt closer to her than anyone else in her life.

She swallowed back the hopelessness of her situation. She'd never yearned for anyone as much as Liam, and the pain of this separation was hurting her far more than what Ivy could ever do to her.

The clean smell of pine needles whiffed past her nose, and she realized she was moving a little higher as the breeze was becoming stronger, but it felt good against her warm skin. She was reasonably fit. Yoga kept her body supple, although it had been a while since she'd last been to class.

There was a bench ahead, and she looked at her watch. She had been traveling for a couple of hours now. As she reached the wooden seat, Amelia took off her rucksack and sat down.

The view was beautiful, tall trees that looked as if they reached the sky, with shadows between the old—and some of them, distorted—trunks. But oh, how amazing they looked—tall, strong, and so full of life. The things they must have seen. If only they could tell their story.

Taking her phone out, she saw that she had a signal. She had dozens of missed calls and several text messages. They were all from Liam. She didn't want to read the text messages. At this point she didn't want to be diverted from what was her plan, and she knew that if she read just one message she would be highly likely to lose the strength she had and needed.

The unbearable knowledge that she had made Liam unhappy was devastating. However, she'd rather do that than have him die because of her. A single tear dropped from her eye, rolling down her cheek and onto the material of her jeans. The agonizing pain that knotted in her stomach almost made her fall to her knees. It was unlike anything she'd ever felt before.

Another tear rolled down her cheek, and she brushed it away with a vigorous swipe. She had to pull herself together. There had been no other choice but for her to leave. Trying to lure Ivy Rossi to her was exhausting and frightening. The woman had to be deranged to cause such insane violence toward her regardless of anyone else who could have been hurt.

Amelia had never liked her. There had always been something completely off about the woman, but she could never put her finger on what. Now she could, and it terrified the hell out of her.

It was miraculous that she was still standing, and if it hadn't been for Liam, she knew she'd probably be dead by now. She missed him, so much more than she thought possible. It felt as though a part of her was missing. A large measure of comfort rolled through her knowing that at least he would be safe now.

Amelia had been two women inside one body. Her alter ego had taken over her life for so long she didn't know if she remembered how to be her. But she felt certain that she could set aside Amelia Bailey and bring back Amelia Rose, even if it would only be for a short while.

****

Ivy Rossi watched the red dot on her phone screen. It had suddenly started to move. She'd tried to make her way toward the house, but it had been too difficult, so she was more than happy when the tracker had led her in another direction. It had stopped again, so Ivy waited for the red dot to bleep.

The main aim for her was to be invisible. What was the point of going to all this trouble and getting caught?

She was patient and would wait as long as it took for her to get her hands on the bitch who'd ruined her son's life.

Angus had been careless, and he was paying for it now. He'd always been the son who'd used his fists first. Her other son, Tony, was the clever one. It had always been that way from the day they were born. Tony was the eldest with only twelve months between them.

Suddenly, her phone started bleeping. Amelia was on the move again. "Fucking fantastic," Ivy murmured as she made the screen bigger so that there was a clear line on the map to see which way she was going.

After the two mistakes she'd already made trying to kill Amelia, she would make damn sure that this time the bitch would not be walking away. Then she could go back to the UK and get on with her life.

The two weapons she had by her were all she would need, and of course the two sticks of dynamite, which she was going to have some fun with. Ivy put those in a pocket with a flap and fastened the Velcro shut off her khaki cargo pants. After slipping the knife down her sock, she put the gun in the waistband of her trousers.

It could be a trap, so she would have to be careful and keep her distance so she could keep an eye out for anything that seemed suspicious. The excitement of the kill was getting her all animated, and she could feel herself moving faster and faster through the growth.

She had to stop and take a breath. Ivy didn't want to fuck it up because she was being careless. Her palms were sweating, and she cleaned them on her trousers. There were no nerves, just exhilaration.

She had no idea if the bitch was on her own or if she had security with her. It would be great if her 'boyfriend' was there, because she'd kill him first and make the bitch watch, and then she'd take her time with the torture she wanted to inflict on Amelia.

Heart racing, Ivy could hardly contain her excitement as she got closer and closer. Finally, she would be able to bring this whole nightmare to an end.

****

Liam kept up with the other men, cursing himself for allowing this to happen. He should have been more aware. He should have known that Amelia would do this. She was protecting all of them by guiding Ivy Rossi in her direction.

Panic slithered down his spine. What if they were too late? Amelia had thought about what she was doing when she had taken the GPS tracker with her. Liam looked at his watch for the hundredth time. Biting back a groan, he followed closely behind Micah, who was in constant contact with the marshals via an earpiece.

Griffin tapped him on the shoulder from behind and he turned and fell into step beside him.

"We'll find her. Micah is one of the best trackers in the business."

"Yeah, but will it be in time?"

"Hey," Griffin said, "always be positive. Nothing good comes from thinking like that."

Liam took a deep breath. "You're right."

They stopped. "The tracks become two sets here, so we can assume that Ivy has Amelia," Micah said.

Liam thought he was going to throw up. All three of them crouched down to look at the map which Micah had spread on a rock.

"There's a cabin about a mile ahead. I'm betting that's where they are," he said as he folded the map and slipped it into his pocket.

"We need to go in quietly until we figure out what this lunatic has planned," Griffin said as he checked his gun.

"I agree," Micah said as he turned to look at Liam.

Liam knew what he was going to ask. "Not a chance, Micah."

"You should really stay behind. But I can see you're determined." Micah shook his head, and his brows knitted together as he pushed his fingers through his short hair. "Can you shoot?" he asked.

"Yes." He'd learned when the wife of a man had shot him in the leg when he'd put her husband who had raped and killed three women in prison for life.

"Here," Micah said, handing Liam a gun. "Take this, and be careful."

Liam nodded and put it in the back waistband of his jeans.

Micah used his radio to let everyone know the coordinates of where they were going and to stay behind them.

"We need to move one and a half clicks south," he said to Griffin.

"Got ya," he uttered.

They continued in the same formation as before, and with each step, Liam could feel his heart rate accelerate. He was no Marine or Navy SEAL like Micah had been. But he'd been through enough scary times to be able to handle himself.

It took approximately ten minutes before they saw a cabin ahead of them. Slowing down, Micah gestured for them to stop, and he took out his binoculars. "There's movement, but I can't see clearly who's in there. Griffin, go around the back of the cabin. Check to see if there's a back door, and if you can see anything. Do not make contact."

Griffin nodded and was gone.

Liam felt the tension in his shoulders every second that he was gone. They were crouched on the ground, and Micah kept looking through the binoculars, checking and re-checking for identification.

"Anything?" Liam asked.

Micah shook his head. "Nothing. I can't even tell if there is more than one person in there."

Griffin came up behind them, Liam didn't even hear him.

"No back door, just two small windows. It looks like there are two people inside. I can hear a female voice. Something is going on in there, and it isn't good. I think we've found them."

Micah nodded. Just then three men approached them from behind, and quicker than a heartbeat, Micah and Griffin had their guns out.

"Hey," one of the men said, holding up his hand. "United States Marshals."

Micah nodded at them. "There's no time to waste. Here's the plan." He kept his voice low. "There's only one floor, and from what we can see, there's three rooms. Two people in this area." Micah drew a plan on some paper. "I'm not a hundred percent sure if this is the perp and her victim, so we will have to take things as they come."

They all studied his plan before handing the paper back to him.

Micah looked at Liam. "I don't suppose I can persuade you to—"

"No," Liam said, not giving him a chance to finish.

"Okay, you stay behind me, do you understand?"

Liam nodded. But there wasn't anything he wouldn't do for Amelia, even if it meant risking his own life.

Micah motioned for them to get into their positions. But before they could advance a door opened, and Amelia came out onto the porch with Ivy Rossi following behind her. But it wasn't that which made his heart stop. It was the dynamite strapped to Amelia's body.

****

This was what Amelia had wanted, for the whole thing to be over. Just Ivy and her. She'd run away so no one else would be involved. But as she looked in front of her she saw Liam standing about twenty-five feet away behind Micah.

Oh God, and she had dynamite attached to her body, a thin wire running around her waist and in Ivy's hands.

She could feel the blood inside her mouth where she had been kicked in the face. Amelia did not doubt that her face was black and blue from bruising. She'd taken one hell of a beating from Ivy.

But that was the least of her problems. Her hands were tied behind her back with plastic cable ties. They dug into her skin because of how tight they were.

At her back was a gun, and she could feel the end poking her in the ribs from behind. The woman was so clearly unhinged it was a wonder she wasn't already locked up. Amelia's heart rate was beating out of control.

Why, oh why, did Liam have to follow her? She'd wanted to deal with this on her own. It was no one else's problem but hers. How had she managed to make such a mess of everything?

"Don't come any closer, or you'll be finding bits of her all around you." Ivy spoke beside her as she showed them the wire attached to the explosives.

"Please," Amelia whispered. "Don't hurt anyone else because of me."

"Stop sniveling. You should have thought out your plan a bit better than this." Ivy pulled her hair back so hard that it jerked her head. "Because of you, my son is sitting in a prison…for life. You have to pay for that."

"Ouch." She winced in pain. A tear fell onto her split lip, and the salt hurt like hell as she licked it off and the metallic taste of blood swathed her mouth.

"Don't be such a baby, or you'll get a lot more than a beaten face."

Out of the side of her eye, Amelia thought she saw movement. To try to stop Ivy from seeing it, she pulled herself from her hold to distract her.

"Hey, bitch, do that again and I'll kill you right here in front of your boyfriend."

Wasn't that what she was going to do anyway?

"Ivy, why don't you just let her go?" Liam shouted, and if she wasn't mistaken, he was getting closer.

"Oh, he speaks," Ivy said sarcastically. "This is the man who is coming to save you." She laughed, and it reminded Amelia of a witch's cackle. "If you move one inch closer, I'm going to light this fuse quicker than you'll be able to get to her." To prove a point Ivy flicked the lighter she had on and off.

Liam stopped in his tracks. Amelia could see the look of fear on his face. A burst of panic launched inside her stomach.

"Listen, Ivy, I'm a criminal law attorney, a good one. If you let Amelia go, I'll help defend you."

"Oh, I'm sure you will," Ivy said sarcastically. "You're just a liar like all of them. Sheriffs, FBI, cops, every single one of you. This is only gonna end one way, and if I have to die with this bitch, I will."

Amelia didn't know why, but she knew when Ivy was going to light that fuse. Ivy whispered in her ear, "Rot in hell, honey." And a second later the lighter flicked on, the flame wavering in the slight breeze, and in what seemed like slow motion she lit the fuse just as a shot rang out.

"Amelia!" she heard Liam shout. But she couldn't do anything but watch the fuse wire sizzle as it moved toward the dynamite. Just at the side of her Ivy lay dead, blood spilling out of the wound to her head.

There was a distinct ammonia smell, she could taste it in her mouth, and the feeling of being a firecracker was prevalent in her mind and body. It seemed to last forever, but it was only seconds before she was thrown to the ground by someone and the end of the fuse was cut off before it lit the dynamite.

"OMG, OMG," she breathed out.

The person who was lying on top of her was…Liam.

"Amelia, honey." As he pulled her up, someone else, Micah, was undoing the explosives from her body and took them away.

They were surrounded by other men. Through the harrowing fear of surviving the neurotic retribution of a woman who'd taken it upon herself to seek revenge for a man who should never be let out of prison, Amelia wasn't sorry that Ivy was dead.

"You're safe now," Liam said to her.

Looking up into his eyes, she tried to blink the tears back. He cradled her face in his hands and pressed his lips to her forehead, and she couldn't help the yelp of relief that came from her.

Micah leaned in and undid the cable ties from her wrist.

Everything that was going on around them became distant. She didn't have to hide her feelings anymore, and she wrapped her arms around Liam, and he lifted her feet from the ground.

Liam let out a soft groan as he tightened his hold. "Jesus, Amelia, I could have lost you."

"You were so brave. You could have been hurt. What the hell were you doing?" she whispered.

"I couldn't think of anything but what Ivy Rossi was doing to you."

Running her hands up and down his back, she kissed him full on the mouth, and the tremor that rolled through her finally settled to a heartbeat as he returned her kiss.

"Hey, you two, get a room."

They both looked up to see Griffin grinning at them.

"It's over," she murmured.

"It sure is, baby."

"I love you," Amelia said.

Liam gazed back at her, and his blue eyes misted with tears as they focused on her.

"I love you so, so much," he said adoringly.

Epilogue

Amelia wrapped her coat around her as Liam looked out of the hotel room window. The snow was coming down fast in large flakes. The trees outside were white, and the roads were only clear because of the gritters.

Being back in London for the first time in many years was exhilarating. This had been her home, where she'd been born. Her mum was buried in the cemetery down the street, which was her whole reason for being there. To let her mum know she was fine—she'd survived and she was happy.

Liam came up behind her and gathered her in his arms. She leaned her head back and covered his hands with her own. The misery that had clung to her like a dark cloud had been removed, and she didn't mind admitting she felt like a new woman. Finally, she was allowed to move forward.

It felt like a dream that she was here, but she knew it was real, as real as the man standing behind her. She had been on an emotional roller coaster, and this was the final installment of her former life. The part where she said goodbye and started a new chapter with the man she loved.

"Are you ready?" he asked her.

She nodded and turned around. "I can't believe it's all over, and you and I are together."

Liam leaned down and kissed her softly on the lips.

He always knew when she needed gentleness, just the same way he was able to know her need for passion.

"Come on," he said, taking her hand.

She picked up the flowers for her mum's grave and turned to him

"I'll love you forever," she said.

"Always and forever until the end of time," he replied as he gripped her fingers with his, giving her the comfort and commitment for their lifelong love.

A word about the author…

Author Dilys J Carnie loves to write, usually contemporary romance, sometimes with a bit of suspense thrown in for good measure.

If she isn't in her office pounding the keys, she's settling into her favorite chair to read a book from one of her many best-loved authors.

Dilys is the proud mum of two grown-up children and two grandchildren.

She lives on the coast of Wales in the United Kingdom.

It is only two hundred steps to the beach from her home, where she lives with her cat Molly.

www.dilysjcarnie.com

9 781509 254170